T0354769

HUMAN NATURE

HUMAN NATURE

Peter Kaufman

HUMAN NATURE

Copyright © 2019 Peter Kaufman.

All rights reserved. No part of this book may be used or reproduced by any means, graphic, electronic, or mechanical, including photocopying, recording, taping or by any information storage retrieval system without the written permission of the author except in the case of brief quotations embodied in critical articles and reviews.

iUniverse books may be ordered through booksellers or by contacting:

iUniverse
1663 Liberty Drive
Bloomington, IN 47403
www.iuniverse.com
1-800-Authors (1-800-288-4677)

Because of the dynamic nature of the Internet, any web addresses or links contained in this book may have changed since publication and may no longer be valid. The views expressed in this work are solely those of the author and do not necessarily reflect the views of the publisher, and the publisher hereby disclaims any responsibility for them.

Any people depicted in stock imagery provided by Getty Images are models, and such images are being used for illustrative purposes only.
Certain stock imagery © Getty Images.

ISBN: 978-1-5320-7908-5 (sc)
ISBN: 978-1-5320-7909-2 (e)

Library of Congress Control Number: 2019910506

Print information available on the last page.

iUniverse rev. date: 07/25/2019

Fragment: Giant Malt George

It was something Lefty Murdoch used to say over and over...that the smartest thing he ever did was to hire George Fisher. George worked the soda fountain-lunch counter at Murdoch's Pharmacy-drugstore located a couple of blocks up the hill from the pier, on the southwest corner of Center Street and Manhattan Avenue, in Manhattan Beach, California. George also did general cleaning, merchandise display set-ups and inventory control. When work at the soda fountain slacked off completely, George ran the cash register by the front door of the drugstore.

Lefty Murdoch pitched in the Pacific Coast League for the San Francisco Seals from 1928 to the fall of 1935 when he injured his shoulder and retired from baseball. It was early in 1936 in the depths of the Depression when Lefty moved to Manhattan Beach and bought the pharmacy-drugstore at an estate liquidation sale.

Lefty loved all types of sports and that's why, in July 1938, he hired George Fisher, right after George had graduated in June from Redondo Union High School. It was in George's senior year, '37-'38, when the Sea Hawks won championships in football and basketball in both the Bay League and the Southern Division of the California Interscholastic Federation. George was a star on both of those championship teams. He also played first base on the Sea Hawk's baseball team.

George really brought in a crowd at the drugstore. Although enormously popular, he also made the best malts, milk shakes and sodas anywhere in the South Bay...especially the malts. And it was those super rich, thick, large malts that earned George Fisher the nickname, "Giant Malt George." George's expertise also let Lefty raise the price for malts from 20 to 25 cents, a hefty price in 1938.

During the summer, the drugstore was open from nine in the morning to seven in the evening, six days a week, and from ten in the morning to four in the afternoon on Sundays. After Labor Day, hours were nine to five, six days, and closed on Sunday. Lefty always opened the store every morning unless he had a "situation." He never explained what a "situation" was, and Giant Malt George never asked. But he knew when a situation came up, because that was when Lefty gave him his store key the night before and told him to open in the morning.

At the end of October in '38, Lefty gave Giant Malt George a key of his own…not only were situations increasing…but Lefty now had confidence George could run everything smoothly until Lefty or the pharmacist, Larry Carter, arrived.

And, the sports crowd that congregated at the drugstore at nine-fifteen on weekdays kept an eye on things every day but Saturday and Sunday. The sports crowd were all friends of Lefty. The group included Big Al, a retired attorney and widower; Turk, a former high school football coach; Dutch, a retired career army officer; Rocco, a CPA; Walt, an ocean-going tug skipper "on-the-beach" because of an injury; and Doc Cole, a long-time Manhattan Beach doctor.

Big Al always arrived for coffee before the others, promptly at nine. He and Giant Malt George had a special understanding: to get the day started correctly, Big Al drank his first cup of coffee, and only the first, laced with either Four Roses or Three Feathers. Big Al supplied a pint of lacing which George kept hidden in a paper bag behind the soda fountain counter.

Like clockwork every third Friday, George said to Big Al, "We're running short of inventory."

Big Al, a notorious, to-the-penny, record-keeper, always nodded in recognition of George's precise measuring skills: an ounce a day. Later, Big Al would bring in a new pint, wrapped in a paper bag, and hand it to George. It became a game: Big Al always counted on his own and then waited for George to remind him. That reassured Big Al he was not supplying lacing for anyone else's coffee. To say it straight, Giant Malt George was exactly Big Al's kind of guy: honest, prompt, careful, detailed, and well-liked by everyone. What's more, he also made great tuna salad sandwiches that Big Al paid for at coffee to be made later. After the sandwiches were made up fresh at two PM, then George took them down to the pier where Big Al was fishing. George often brought along some sandwiches for himself, and he and Big Al ate a late lunch together. Big Al's Monday to Friday set routine never varied.

When the rest of the sports crowd assembled each weekday morning, whatever was hot in sports was the topic for the day: baseball, college football or basketball, horse racing at Del Mar or down in Mexico at Agua Caliente, or the new craze...professional wrestling at the Olympic Auditorium with Ernie Dusek and "Man Mountain Dean." It was the latter topic that caused the most heated discussions: was the wrestling real or just a show? And, as usual, everyone tried to get Lefty to tell stories about his pitching days and experiences with the Seals.

"Don't get me involved, no time to talk baseball today," Lefty always said.

"Come on, Lefty," Turk pleaded on one occasion. "Today's hot question is: What's easier? To pitch in one of the Coast League's Tuesday-to-Saturday-night games, or in one of the doubleheader day games on Sunday?"

Lefty stopped, looked at Turk, and in his usual evasive manner replied, "Depends on the ball park, Turk, and the time of year. It can be the lights and cooler weather at night or it's the sun, shadows and maybe heat and humidity during the day. Is that any help?"

The sports group groaned in unison as Lefty never helped settle a hot baseball question. Then Rocco asked Giant Malt George what he thought, since he also played baseball for the Sea Hawks.

"Never played at night, Rocco, and, of course, I wasn't a pitcher so I'm no help," he replied. But George wondered when the guys would figure out Lefty was never going to give any kind of opinion that might cut off the debates, annoy one of the guys, or get the sports gang upset enough to stop meeting at his drugstore.

Sometimes the topic focused on the good old days in the Coast League: the caliber of play was great, guys were going up to the majors, Lefty pitched for the Seals, and Joe and Dominic DiMaggio were both playing at the same time in the league. Lefty usually ignored the question, shrugged his shoulders and walked away.

But once Lefty did say, "Joe and Dominic are great, no doubt about it. Remember, in 1931 when Joe was just 18 and had the 61-game hitting streak for the Seals? You watch; he'll do something like that again while

3

he's playing for the Yankees." Lefty's comment caused a week of heated conversation.

In the fall of '38 when high school started after Labor Day, some of the kids coming home got off the bus at Highland and Center and walked the block down the hill to Murdoch's. That's when Giant Malt George went into action: Cokes, sodas, floats, milk shakes and for the few who could afford it, one of his famous malts. Another of George's talents was to carry on a half-dozen separate conversations with different groups of kids, all at the same time while he worked…and he always remembered what all the talk was about and what everyone said.

Because the Depression made it critical to avoid clothes competition, all girls at Redondo High had to wear plain, dark-blue skirts and white blouses. Any jacket or sweater was okay, and so for the very boy-conscious girl, the sweater made a big difference.

So, girls came trooping into Murdoch's to show off their sweaters, to see if any sundries were on special sale, to have a Coke or just to visit with Giant Malt George…and not necessarily in that order. There was no doubt about the central attraction, Giant Malt George. He had dated a couple of senior girls, Judy Foster and Lynne Hughes, during that fall in '38. Occasionally he and his basketball teammate, Jack Hill, an All Bay League forward, double-dated and went to the Venice Ballroom when one of the name bands like Benny Goodman was playing there. Jack had a car, a '32 V-8 Ford Coupe, with a rumble seat. Giant Malt George did not have a car. Admission to the Ballroom was 50 cents each, so the guys had to save up, as well as pay for gas and Cokes.

When the high school sweater girls came into the drugstore, the pharmacist, Larry Carter, always skipped out from behind the pharmacy counter at the back of the store and visited with them. Larry made no secret he enjoyed all the young high school girls that Giant Malt George attracted, and Larry usually had his arm around any one of them not lucky enough to have moved quickly out of his way. The girls called him, "Clutching Carter".

In late June of '39 Giant Malt George started dating Carolyn Hodge, who would be a senior in the fall. Carolyn was a very modest, serious young girl who loved to read and talk to George at length about what she learned from everything she read. She lived right on the Strand between 30th and 31st Streets, not far from George's mother's house. Carolyn was full of fun, enjoyed charming Giant Malt George with stories she made up and, without a doubt, was very drawn to him. She told her friends, "George Fisher is far more than just a former high school star athlete. In the future, he will show it. You just watch." Carolyn was certainly no wallflower. She was very athletic and loved to swim. Carolyn was also tall, had a beautiful, graceful figure and when she and Giant Malt George went down to the beach, she wore a form-fitting, all wool Catalina swimsuit. George remarked once to his mother Helen, that Carolyn's swimsuit was really an attention-getter at the beach. "I think it's better for the girl's gym pool at Redondo High than for the beach," George said.

Helen laughed heartily. "Oh, George, she's just been blessed by Mother-Nature. You're a very lucky young man."

"You're right, Mom, I am lucky, in so many ways. We've been able to stay on here in Manhattan Beach all these years. My sports ability did good things for me in high school, and I was able to get a job in these tough times. And all your years of hard work and sacrifice for us. Now I not only have a wonderful, beautiful girlfriend, made great friends at the drugstore with some older guys who come in early every morning and talk sports, drink coffee and have a donut, but I've met a man I especially like called Big Al. He's easy to talk to and knows a lot. And I'm learning how to run a soda fountain-lunch counter like it was my own business."

When George left the house, Helen thought about what her son had said and what he didn't know about their life. She had had a long struggle after George's father, Henry, deserted her in 1929 when George was only nine. That was when the Depression began, and she got the cocktail waitress job, only because she was so attractive. Oh, the risks she took to make barely enough to live on, to pay someone to watch George, and to be able to make their monthly house payment. This house: the only thing saved out of the marriage and it saved her and George as well. Her big break was beauty school, and then getting the beauty parlor job in Redondo Beach right at the end of the Pacific Electric streetcar line. That made it so easy getting to work. Oh, that wonderful beauty parlor job which was located next to the only exclusive Women's Wear shop in Redondo…right where women who could afford it went to the beauty parlor first and then shopping. Also, because Redondo was twice as large as Manhattan Beach it meant more customers and tips. Yes, what George didn't know about their life, especially hers! Every woman has to keep some secrets, and sometimes you get lucky and things do work out for the best, Helen said to herself.

Early in September of '39, a terrible heat wave engulfed all of southern California for weeks. Temperatures exceeded one hundred degrees in Los Angeles and nearly ninety degrees at the beaches. After the heat wave broke, gale force winds and heavy rains began. Floods, destruction and high seas resulted. Some of the beach piers were heavily damaged all the way from Santa Monica to Redondo Beach. The early sports crowd stuck out the bad weather, but the topic of the weather soon grew tiresome and it changed. The German army had invaded Poland, which some said showed that years of appeasing Hitler proved appeasement was a disaster. The sports crowd was evenly divided between the positions 'stay out of Europe's problems' and 'we need to do something'. No one was able to say with any certainty what that something should be.

Despite the heat wave, rains, winds, flooding and a general gloomy mood, Big Al's poker group, The Ace of Clubs, continued to meet every third weekend on Saturday night. Lefty and the sports group belonged. Everyone chipped in for food and Giant Malt George made up dozens of sandwiches for the meeting. Big Al kept count: food costs as well as winnings or losses...to the penny. George heard the beverages served were not from his specialty list.

Thanksgiving Day 1939 came and went. Lefty asked Giant Malt George the following Friday morning to begin setting up the Christmas merchandise displays and to come in on this Sunday if he couldn't finish everything by Saturday. Lefty showed George all the Christmas merchandise shipment boxes stored in the basement. Lefty said he wanted displays for the Evening in Paris perfume packaging, the candle putt-putt boats, the Felix the Cat and Popeye the Sailorman wind-up boats, the Wonder Auto friction power car, Picolo and Talisman Bears, Shirley Temple dolls, a rack for the Barrel Tumblers and a big Kodak Verichrome film layout. To set up all these displays, George needed to take down regular displays to make room. So, he said to Lefty if he didn't finish on Saturday, he would come in extra early Sunday 'cause he could only work until ten, or a little after on Sunday as he and Jack Hill were going out for a last minute, surprise birthday celebration.

"Whose birthday?" Lefty asked.

"Mine."

"When is it?" Lefty said.

"It was on the 25th," George said.

"Hey, that's the same day as Joe DiMaggio's birthday. What are you going to do?"

"Gosh, I didn't know that. Well, Jack Hill and I are going to the saltwater Plunge in Redondo."

"Okay. Where's Carolyn? Isn't she going, too?" Lefty asked.

"She's over in Palos Verdes spending Thanksgiving vacation visiting her grandparents. She'll be back late Sunday night for school on Monday."

"I know you'll miss her but have a great time, anyway," Lefty said.

At his usual time the following Monday morning, Giant Malt George walked down from his house to the Strand at 28th Street and along the Strand to the pier. Then he turned left on Center and started to walk up the hill to the drugstore. As he neared Manhattan Avenue, he saw all three of Manhattan Beach's Police Department squad cars, plus an L.A. County sheriff's car, parked every which way at the corner on Manhattan Avenue near the door to the drugstore.

"Gosh, there must be something wrong," he yelled running the rest of the way up the hill. Lefty Murdoch was standing outside the drugstore on the sidewalk. Giant Malt George called out, "Lefty, what's wrong?"

"We've been robbed, and Larry Carter is dead!"

"Dead?" George shouted.

"Yes, dead! And some money's gone." Lefty said.

"How? Larry was here and okay when I left yesterday! And what money?"

Right then, Manhattan Beach's only criminal investigator, Detective Russ 'Red' Owens, came out of the drugstore's door. Red had been promoted to Detective after he completed a two-year-long, every weekend resident training program at the Los Angeles Police Academy. Red shouted loudly, "Don't say anything more, Lefty. I'll take over now. And I want you to remember, write it down, please…exactly what George Fisher said as he came up the hill and to the door here."

"Sure, Red, but why?" Lefty said in a puzzled tone.

7

"I'll explain later, Lefty. Okay, Fisher, let's get started. I want a complete, detailed description of your activities and whereabouts since yesterday morning, Sunday the 27th. I've got my police stenographer here and she's ready to take down everything, and I mean everything, you say," he added.

"I'm all set, Red," Susan Worth said, holding up a stenographer pad and pencil.

"Let's go then. Did you come to the drugstore yesterday, Fisher?"

"Yes, I did. But what's this all about, Red?"

"I'll ask the questions, hot shot, you just answer. What time did you arrive?"

"Around seven in the morning."

"How did you get in?"

"I have a drugstore key and let myself in."

"Why were you here?"

"To clean up and to finish setting up the displays of Christmas merchandise."

"Who told you to do all this?"

"Lefty. All you have to do is ask him."

"Just answer, hot shot. Don't add anything. You mean this was scheduled work time?"

"Yes."

"Why on Sunday?"

"After school starts and the summer crowds are gone, we close on Sunday. When Lefty asks me, I show up Sunday mornings to do extra work or to clean up. Extra work. Like inventory count or setting up merchandise displays."

"Slow down a bit, Red, I'm getting behind," Susan pleaded.

"Just shut up and do your job, Susan. Okay, again now, Fisher, so you come here every Sunday after school starts?"

"No, like I said, only when Lefty asks me to come in and do clean up or other jobs."

"Just a simple 'yes' or 'no', hot shot, I don't want a big explanation."

"Sure, Red."

"So you are completely familiar with the setup at the drugstore on Sunday and whether anyone else is going to come in?"

"No."

"What do you mean, 'No'?"

"I mean I'm here doing the work Lefty tells me to do. I don't know if anyone else is going to be here."

"Okay, so then someone coming in you don't expect, maybe Lefty or Larry, is a surprise?"

"Yes, I guess you could call that sort of a surprise."

"So, you didn't know Larry Carter was coming in yesterday, on Sunday?"

"No."

"Sort of upset your plans, eh!"

"What do you mean, Red?"

"Hey, once again, Fisher, I'll ask the questions. You just answer them, got it?"

"Yeah, sure."

"Do you have your key to the drugstore, now?"

"No."

"Where is it?"

"I gave it to Larry Carter."

"Why did you do that?"

"He asked for it."

"Why?"

"Larry came in around nine, while I was working, to make up a prescription. Then there were a couple of phone calls, and I heard Larry agree with Doc Cole to fill some prescriptions for pick up first thing on Monday morning. Sometime before ten, Mrs. Carter came to the door. I had to open it for her with my key because Larry's keys were not in the door lock. She complained to Larry it was nearly ten, that she had to be in Santa Monica by eleven, and that she had to walk from Morningside Drive, and now back, because Larry had the car keys. I saw Larry give her some keys and Mrs. Carter stomped out."

"But why did Larry need your keys, then?"

"I guess his drugstore key must be on the same key ring as the car key."

"That's not answering my question, hot shot. Why did he need your keys?"

"I had to leave, my work was done. Larry wasn't through. He had all the extra work he got from Doc Cole by phone. Larry said he'd lock up if I gave him my key. I could get it back on Monday at work."

"Don't you need your keys on Monday, Fisher?"

"Not usually."

"Why not?"

"Because on Mondays and other days I always come in just before nine which is my start time. Lefty opens between eight and eight-thirty unless Lefty says he will be late, and then I come in earlier than usual and open up."

"Does Lefty ever give you his keys to open up?"

"He used to give me his key to the front door but last October he got me my own key."

"So, if most of the time Lefty opens up regularly on Mondays, why would you need a key on Monday?"

"Like I said, Red, I don't. On most days I leave my key at home, so I don't risk losing it. I only bring the key to work when I have to open up."

"Okay, so you could give Larry your keys on Sunday because Lefty usually opens on Monday?"

"Right."

"Did Lefty change the locks when he bought the pharmacy? How many people have keys to the drugstore, Fisher?"

"I don't know the answer to either question, Red. You'll have to ask Lefty."

"Okay, forget about the locks for now. How many people do you know have keys?"

"Three."

"And they are...?"

"Lefty, Larry and me. Say, what's all this stuff about keys, Red?"

"I'll tell you what, star athlete. When Lefty arrived this morning, the store was locked. He found Larry dead inside. We found no keys anywhere. Not on Larry or hanging from the inside door lock where Lefty says it's Larry's habit to leave keys. No sign of forced entry here or at the basement, storage area door to the alley. Got it, Fisher?"

"Not really, especially about the basement door."

"What do you mean, Fisher?"

"Well, the basement door is locked with a padlock on the inside and only Lefty has a key for that."

"Your key won't open the padlock?"

"NO, just like I said."

"Let's not get cute, Fisher. Okay, when did you leave the drugstore, hot shot?"

"Just after ten."

"How do you remember the time?"

"From the clock over the soda fountain counter. And, as I said before, when Mrs. Carter came to the door, she said to Larry it was ten o'clock, and he knew she had to drive to Santa Monica to visit her sister for a couple of days and be there to join a group for lunch."

"Okay, skip Mrs. Carter. What happened next, Fisher?"

"Larry said he was working on some prescriptions Doc Cole phoned to him. One was for Julia Brown's young son, Tom, for a cough. And Larry asked me to walk over to the Brown's and deliver it."

"Where do they live?"

"On the Strand between 7th and 6th Streets."

"What did you do?"

"I gave Larry my key. He gave me the prescription. We both walked to the front door. He opened it and I left."

"Did you turn around and see Larry lock the door behind you?"

"No."

"Did you hear the door lock click behind you?"

"I don't remember, but the door lock does make a loud sound when locked."

"Did you see what he did with your keys?"

"No, like I said, I didn't turn around but probably he left my key in the lock like he always does."

"So, you don't know for a fact that he left your keys in the lock?"

"No, but I only have a single key, Red, not a bunch of keys."

"Okay, Fisher, you're telling me you gave Larry your key, a single key, to the drugstore and left the drugstore just after ten to deliver a prescription to the Brown's."

"Yes, that's it."

"Which way did you walk to the Brown's?"

"Well. I turned right, walked down Manhattan Avenue to 6th turned right down to the Strand, and then right to the Brown's."

"Are you sure that's the way you went, Fisher?"

"Yes, I'm sure."

"You didn't walk down to the pier first?"

"No, why would I do that?"

"Just answer my questions, hot shot, and don't try to question me."

"Okay, Red."

"What time did you arrive at the Brown's?"

"No later than about ten fifteen or so."

"Why can't you give me the precise time as you have been doing all along?"

"I don't have a watch."

"Okay, so what did you do then?"

"I walked down the stairs to the Red Car stop on the beach at 7th Street to get the ten-thirty to Redondo Beach."

"What were you wearing?"

"Tan cords, my good blue shirt and my Redondo letter sweater. Oh yeah, and I was carrying my swim trunks rolled up in a towel."

"Are those clothes at your home?"

"Sure, they're hanging in my closet, except for the trunks that are still on the clothesline out back."

"I'm going to have officer Murphy pick them up when you go home, got it?"

"Sure, Red, but when do I get everything back? I need the clothes to wear."

"I'll be telling you what and when you will get stuff back, Fisher."

"What's this all about, Red?"

"I'll ask the questions, Fisher. What did you do in Redondo?"

"Met my basketball buddy, Jack Hill, and we went to the saltwater Plunge."

"And after that? Are you getting all this, Susan?"

"Yes, Red, I'm getting it all," Susan quickly replied.

"After the Plunge, we walked to Cid's in the amusement area. We bought a couple of hamburgers and then walked over to the Fox movie theater for the Sunday matinee at two o'clock."

"Were you on time for the start of the show?"

"Yes. Jack has a wristwatch."

"How can you afford all this, Fisher?"

"Because Lefty paid me on Friday. The Plunge costs a quarter, the hamburgers fifteen cents each, the movie a quarter and the Red Car a nickel each way. I spent ninety cents."

"Okay, Mr. Precise, and how much does Lefty pay you?"

"Fifty dollars a month plus lunches, and I give my mom half of my pay."

"Well, aren't you just the generous guy, Mr. Star Athlete! What did you see at the movie?"

"It was a Marx Brothers special double feature: "A Night at the Opera" and "A Day at the Races" plus a Mickey Mouse cartoon and the Movietone News."

"When did the movie let out?"

"Around six o'clock."

"What did you do then?"

"Jack got his car and went home. He lives in south Redondo, up toward Hollywood Riviera. I got the last Red Car at six-thirty and went home."

"I didn't ask about Jack, Fisher, just answer what you did. Now, did you get off at the pier or 28th Street?"

"28th Street."

"You're sure you didn't stop and go out on the pier?"

"Why would I go out on the pier? No, I went straight home."

"For the last time, I'll ask the questions, hot shot. Was you mother home when you arrived?"

"Yes."

"What time was that?"

"About seven-fifteen or so. Mom was listening to the radio, "I Love a Mystery," the serial with Jack, Doc and Reggie."

"Let me stop here for a moment, Fisher, to warn you that you'd better be telling the truth because the Manhattan Beach police, and especially me, are going to check out, six ways from Sunday, every last detail of your alibi."

"What's an alibi, Red?"

"It's the bullshit story of what you say you were doing when the crime occurred."

"What do you mean, bullshit story, Red?"

"Wise up, Mr. Star Athlete, you are our prime suspect!"

"Me? What do you mean, prime suspect? What happened here? I sure don't know."

"Don't make me laugh! Like you don't know, Mr. Star Athlete?"

"No, I don't know, Red, I just got here, remember?"

"Don't get smart with me, Fisher. Larry Carter is lying in there dead with his head smashed in; just where you left him. If I had my way, I'd lock you up right now."

"What in the world are you talking about, Red… 'Just where I left him, and you'd lock me up right now'?"

"You'll find out, hot shot. But a couple more questions. Does Lefty leave money in that cash register behind the soda fountain counters when he closes up in the evening?"

"Maybe, but he could put it there when he opens up in the morning. You'll have to ask Lefty to see what he does. I don't know."

"Okay, let's cover the "maybe" part. How much money is there if money is there when you come in?"

"It varies; Lefty leaves some bills, usually a few ones, and some change so I can start the week or the next day. I find the money when I ring up my first sale in the morning. But as I said, I don't know when he puts the money in the soda fountain cash register."

"So, Lefty actually counts it all out and puts it in the register?"

"Yes."

"Did you find money in the cash register yesterday?"

"I never even checked the cash register yesterday, Red, because we weren't open for business. I was just there to finish the Christmas displays."

"That's a good one, Fisher, 'You never even checked the cash register yesterday'! Do you verify the amount on mornings?"

"No. How can I verify an amount if I don't know what the amount is to verify, Red? But I do count what's there."

"Okay, Fisher. Do you handle larger amounts of money for the drugstore?"

"What do you mean?"

"I mean, who orders and pays for food, milk, Coke syrup, and stuff like that?"

"Lefty does all that. We have deliveries from Van de Kamps for all the baked goods, from Adohr for butter, milk, cream, and ice cream, from Coca Cola plus some other big outfits for cold cuts and the like. Those big deliveries are early Monday morning and again during the week, especially in the summer. Things like donuts come every day. If we run out, and for anything else, Lefty gets everything from Moore's Market just down the street. I usually go over to Moore's and pick everything up, but Lefty pays all those bills. All I handle is money for sales at the soda fountain-lunch counter and, occasionally, I help out at the cash register up front when there is no business at the soda fountain counter."

"So, you do use more than one cash register?"

"Yes."

"Do you stay late? Maybe when Lefty goes home early, and then you handle all the money?"

"No, Lefty has Mrs. Carter come in when he leaves early on weekdays, to cover during peak periods, and to handle any money. I also know many women customers come in when Mrs. Carter will be there to wait on them, and she handles all those sales even if I'm still there. I go home at four…no food is served after that and the soda fountain is closed."

"How long have you worked here?"

"About a year and a half."

"When did you start?"

"July, right after graduation."

"Just give me the year, Fisher."

"1938. But what's all this asking about money? You are saying there isn't any money in my soda fountain register now?"

"Right you are, Mr. Star Athlete. And how many times is your cash register short of the money that should be there?"

"I don't know at all. Lefty handles all the registers at the end of each day. Maybe the soda fountain cash register is off a couple of cents, or over now and then, but I'm not the only one who rings up sales and makes change there."

"You can just bet I'll be checking that out too, Fisher."

Lefty came to the front door, interrupted and asked Giant Malt George to come in and see if anything was missing since he had the best idea about the general merchandise inventory. Lefty said everything in the pharmacy section looked okay, especially all narcotics for prescriptions. Red Owens objected. Said no walk-through until the L.A. County Sheriff's photographer was finished. Lefty insisted, saying it was his drugstore, not

Red's, and he would decide what his employee, Giant Malt George, was going to do.

As all three of them made a quick tour of the drugstore, George said everything looked all right to him except for the Evening in Paris cardboard box display at the front of the store, and the big Voit inflatable beach ball metal rack at the rear near the soda fountain. Both displays were tipped over and their contents lay strewn on the floor. The store reeked of Evening in Paris perfume. Giant Malt George said the only way to be certain was to count everything and to include all the broken blue perfume bottles. Red insisted that no one pass the Voit ball rack mess at the far end of the soda fountain area where Larry Carter lay. George saw dried blood on Larry's head, and at the bases of some of the soda fountain stools where they were fixed to the floor. That was where the Sheriff's Crime scene photographer continued taking pictures.

By now a large crowd had collected outside the drugstore including all the members of the early-morning sports group. Red Owens told officer Murphy to go out and tell everyone to clear the area and that the drugstore would be closed temporarily until the police finished their work.

Red, Lefty and Giant Malt George walked up to the front of the store. Red signaled for Susan Worth to join them, turned to George Fisher and continued his questioning. "Let me go over a special point, Fisher. Did anyone else hear Larry Carter ask to borrow your drugstore key?"

"No. Larry's wife was gone when he asked for the key and, like I said, there was no one else in the store but us."

"So, the part about the key, it's just your story, eh!"

"NO Red, it's not just MY story. I gave Larry my key after Mrs. Carter took his keys and left the drugstore. I took the prescription, left the drugstore, delivered it…and from what you say, the drugstore was locked this morning. I never came back here until this morning. Why should I? The Christmas displays were all set up…my extra work was done."

"Don't shout at me, hot shot! Sure, the drugstore was locked, because you never lent Larry your key since there was no need to."

"What are you talking about, Red?"

"I mean, Fisher, that for a lousy four bucks and some change you smashed in Larry Carter's head just after ten on Sunday morning, before you left to deliver the prescription to Mrs. Brown. Then calmly, without a care, you spent the rest of the day constructing what you think is an airtight alibi. And I'll bet another four bucks and change, right here and now, that the L.A. County Coroner puts the time of Larry's death yesterday around ten o'clock in the morning. Oh, it all fits, Mr. Star Athlete, and I'm going to nail your ass for it. There will be no more last second, final shot heroics for you this time, hot shot!"

"That's a wild theory, Red Owens, you shouldn't be jumping to conclusions like that," Lefty interjected angrily.

"Jumping to conclusions my ass, Lefty. Fisher here admits he never knew Larry was going to show up Sunday. I believe Fisher was going to pinch the money like he's probably been doing all along. Maybe put it back later, but this time his plan screwed up. And the only way out was to smash Larry's head in. And I bet it all happened when Larry caught hot shot here taking money just before leaving to deliver the Brown prescription. Fisher admits he has access to two of your registers as part of his regular duties. And, Fisher here knows that a set of keys or a key is always left in the door because the only way out of the drugstore is through the front door. And Fisher says he gave his key to Larry, so where is it? The answer, plain as the nose on your face, is that Fisher made the story up…he never gave Larry his key."

"What in the world are you saying, Red Owens? First of all, Giant Malt George doesn't know what our emergency Sunday schedule for the pharmacy is during the year. All the pharmacists in the South Bay are on an emergency rotation schedule for Sundays, or any other day, all year round. All the doctors have the schedule for every day. I have one, too. November 27th was our turn, Doc Cole called Larry Carter for some emergency work, and Larry came in. It's a good thing we have this system, too, because Larry is almost always away on Sundays. He goes out to that gambling ship anchored beyond the three-mile limit. The Rex I think it is called. Larry takes the first Sunday morning water taxi from San Pedro and comes back in on the last taxi to leave The Rex very early Monday morning. Furthermore, Red, I always check the cash registers and there has never, never been any money missing."

Giant Malt George, stunned, stood there disbelieving what Red Owens was saying. He thought, 'I know how much Red Owens hates me because Red's son, Russ Junior, only made the B squads and not the A's for the

Sea Hawks.' George also recalled Red saying…over and over, that the Sea Hawks were so good in '37-'38; they would have won championships without Fisher. And he talked about how Fisher kept his son off the A teams because both were in the same Senior class and played the same positions…right end on the football team and center on the basketball team. George knew the simple truth was that Russ Junior didn't have the talent to make the A teams. Everyone, including Russ Junior, knew it, too. But Red refused to believe it. And it was obvious to Giant Malt George his success caused Red to hate him intensely…but enough to accuse him of killing Larry Carter?

Red turned around, ignored what Lefty said and told officer Murphy, "Take Fisher home, collect the clothes he wore yesterday, and Fisher, don't try to leave town. Also, be here for further questioning tomorrow and after the L.A. County Coroner's report and the lab report on your clothes are available."

Officer Murphy drove George home and collected all the clothing. George sat down in the kitchen and anxiously waited to tell his mother what had happened at the drugstore. When she came home from work, he related detail by detail the events of the morning. Helen was shocked, said all they could do was pray and believe that everything would turn out for the best. George Fisher was not so sure.

About five weeks later, things calmed down. But the high school kids, all except for Carolyn Hodge, abruptly stopped coming into Murdoch's after school. The "Morning Sports Club," as George called it, just as suddenly melted away, and only Big Al was left coming to the drugstore.

Seven weeks after the murder, Giant Malt George made some tuna salad sandwiches and took them down to Big Al on the pier. He asked George to sit down on the bench next to him and recount all the details of what had happened that Sunday at the drugstore. He also wanted to hear exactly what George had said in response to all Red Owens's questions the following Monday morning.

George talked through the whole story again, over and over from beginning to end for Big Al, demonstrating his exceptional memory. He also included Red's theory about what happened, as well as his wild accusations. Big Al asked again and again for details about Mrs. Carter coming to the store, about the keys, about the prescriptions ordered by Doc Cole, about the delivery of the one prescription to Mrs. Brown, about the questions regarding the pier and about what George did the rest of that fateful Sunday.

"What do you think happened?" Giant Malt George finally asked Big Al.

"I don't know, George, but our laws allow for circumstantial evidence. That's where you show opportunity, likely cause, a motive, facts that approach, point to a possible conclusion of what and why things happened, who was responsible and that sort of thing. But in this event at the drugstore, circumstances pertaining to you seem pretty thin to me.

"But, Al, why all those questions about my going out on the pier?" George asked.

"That's part of the circumstantial evidence idea, George. Based on Red saying you never gave Larry Carter your key, he's logically trying to find out if you went out on the pier with no other reasonable explanation of your doing so other than to throw away your key," Big Al replied.

"But that's crazy. I gave Larry Carter my key. I don't know why he didn't have it when Lefty found him, and the police searched him."

"I believe your story, George. Someone who's lying will trip up. Your recollections and retelling of events is remarkably clear and consistent each time you repeat it. That is especially unusual for someone your age and should convince most reasonable people you're telling the truth and have nothing to cover up or have nothing to do with Larry Carter's tragic murder."

"Then what happened, Big Al?"

Big Al shrugged his shoulders and said, "I doubt we'll ever really know," and with that statement, Big Al went back to fishing and eating his lunch. George stood up and slowly walked back up the hill to the drugstore.

A month or so later after his lunch with Big Al on the pier, in March of 1940, Giant Malt George lost his job. Lefty told him he had no choice. Business was way down, and Red Owens was holding daily news sessions with reporters from the "Daily Breeze" ...virtually accusing Lefty of "keeping a murderer on the payroll."

Lefty knew Red was squeezing him hard to get at George, and Lefty soon realized how much Red hated George Fisher. Lefty listened carefully to Red, studying his every gesture...as he had watched batters when he was pitching or following the game from the dugout. Also, Lefty heard Red's tone of voice and saw his angry, vengeful, petty self-centeredness. It was obvious Red Owens was used to getting his own way, would do anything, go to any end, until he got what he wanted. And what he wanted was to get George Fisher.

Lefty was very worried. His weekend "situations" with Hazel Carter and Dolores Owens might come to light. And the last thing Lefty wanted was Red Owens or some reporter from the "Daily Breeze" digging deeper into the lives, motives and opportunities of other people at the drugstore... especially his on the Sunday after Thanksgiving when the murder occurred, and when he spent the day and the night with Hazel Carter in Santa Monica. Lefty figured he had to head things off; he wanted Red Owens investigating only Giant Malt George and no one else.

So, Lefty said to George he was really sorry; he believed George's story about what happened that day, but Lefty just had to do something. Not only was the soda fountain-lunch counter business virtually gone but, Lefty added, he still couldn't get a replacement pharmacist, so he was using Carmel Drug's pharmacist part time to do the few prescriptions still coming in, and the income the store got from it was almost nothing. Again, he told Giant Malt George he was sorry, but to survive he had to do something to get customers back.

The L.A. County Coroner's report and the L.A. police lab report on George Fisher's clothes were detailed verbatim in the "Daily Breeze." According to the coroner Larry Carter died sometime between noon and one PM on Sunday, November 27, 1939. The cause of death was listed as a severely broken neck, and not as a smashed-in head as Red Owens had been telling everyone. George Fisher's clothes evidenced no blood, perfume deposits or stains of any kind. Giant Malt George hoped these reports would convince people he was telling the truth and clear things up in his favor. But Red Owens summarized everything differently. He said a coroner couldn't be totally sure about time of death when the victim had been dead as long as Larry Carter was before he was discovered, and his severely broken neck just proved the savageness of the attack by a strong person such as an athlete. Red Owens said he believed his theories and conclusions about the crime were correct, and he would continue to investigate George Fisher.

During the nearly four months following the murder, Giant Malt George was brought into the police station and questioned over and over and required to repeat his statements again and again. Red Owens kept trying to trip George up or to find a flaw, any flaw or contradiction in Fisher's statements. But every aspect, every facet, especially all the time elements in what George Fisher related were confirmed by a long list of people: Lefty Murdoch; Mrs. Hazel Carter; Mrs. Julia Brown; Dick Hoover and Phil Carpenter Pacific Electric Red Car drivers; Jack Hill; Redondo Salt Water Plunge personnel; Doc Cole, and George's mother Helen. A Richard Ryan also recognized George, who he saw around ten on Sunday morning walking down Manhattan Avenue carrying a package and a rolled-up towel. In addition to the witnesses, L.A. police lab personnel found George's movie ticket stub in his letter sweater pocket. Fox theater personnel confirmed the ticket was issued for the Sunday matinee in question.

Every minute of George Fisher's activities that fateful Sunday and his reputation, character, honesty…his entire life…was examined in painstaking detail and presented to a grand jury both by direct testimony from George Fisher and all other parties. The grand jury did not find enough grounds to return an indictment. It was then that Red Owens announced the investigation of George Fisher would continue its focus being on Sunday, November 27, between the hours of ten o'clock and ten minutes after ten in the morning.

By September 1940, Congress passed the first peacetime draft in the history of the United States. George registered and asked the Selective Service Board to call him up right away. They did. George Fisher said goodbye to his Mom, Carolyn, Big Al...left for the army...and disappeared from Manhattan Beach.

George's mother shared his letters with her friends at the beauty parlor, and with Carolyn. The letters traced in detail his life in the army up to December 7, 1941. After that, censorship meant little detail in his letters, but Helen was able to follow George through North Africa, Sicily, "D" Day, France and Germany. Neither Helen nor any of her friends believed he would survive. Then one day in late 1944 a picture in the newspapers showed General Patton awarding Silver Star Medals, and a Distinguished Service Cross to one soldier...George Fisher. The ugly gossip stopped that Giant Malt George got away from justice, despite the grand jury's decision not to return an indictment, by getting himself drafted into the army.

Sergeant George Fisher pulled his duffel bag off the storage rack at the back of the coach, dragged it out onto the vestibule between the cars, dropped it on the station platform and got off the train. He hoisted the bag up over his left shoulder and walked in the early, cool November morning down the platform toward Union Station, Los Angeles, California. He thought how he'd never expected to live to see southern California again. Two Military Police stopped him, checked his envelope of orders, eyed his rows of combat ribbons and valor decorations and asked him questions about "D" Day. Finally, they shook his hand and told him how to get military transportation on the Pacific Electric Railway to Fort MacArthur, located at the harbor in San Pedro, where he would be paid off and mustered out.

Major Frank Pierce was in a foul mood; the first of the month was always a pain. Annoyed, he glanced up from his desk as the duty clerk handed him some orders and told him a single soldier, a Sergeant George Fisher, was there to be mustered out. With one look, Pierce's mood changed when the Sergeant came in. Never had Pierce encountered a combat infantryman with more decorations than those worn by this Sergeant, who was saluting and standing in front of him. The Major asked George to sit down.

The processing went quickly. The payroll clerk gave George his substantial mustering-out pay and briefly explained GI bill benefits, how to apply for them, and included a booklet listing all the details. Major Pierce had gotten his car and driver from the motor pool and arranged to take civilian George Fisher home to Manhattan Beach.

Pierce shook George's hand and said, "If things don't work out, come back and re-enlist. You'll go up in rank to Master Sergeant, and with your record, you can pick any duty assignment you want."

George thanked him, put his duffel in the trunk of the car, got in the front seat with Private Hughes and was chauffeured home.

Helen Fisher paced anxiously back and forth in the kitchen. She picked up the telegram and read it again for at least the tenth time. 'Mom, Be Home November 1st. George.' Helen was so nervous she'd bitten her fingernails nearly down to the quick. She paced faster. She heard a car stop on Ocean Drive, the narrow street in front of the house, then her son's voice as he thanked someone for the lift home. Helen ran out the front door and threw herself into her son's outstretched arms. She began to sob. George was home for the first time in over five years.

George and Helen stayed up all night talking about life in the army. Finally, George sacked out about five in the morning. Around noon, Helen baked a ham with sweet potatoes and all the fixings. By early afternoon, George still slept. About three in the afternoon, Helen awakened him, and they talked again at the dinner table.

"You never wrote very much about what went on here after I left."

"I thought it best not to, son. Why fill up my letter with unhappy news?"

George said, "Well, what about some of the people at the drugstore, Mom? Especially Lefty, Big Al and Hazel Carter? And what ever happened to Red Owens?"

"Lefty sold the drugstore and moved up to San Francisco in 1941 nearly a year to the day after you joined the army. His business was never successful after he fired you, the high school kids continued to stay away and, of course, the boys you knew at Redondo High had all graduated and scattered to the winds when the war started. Your friend Jack Hill was killed in the Pacific. And in the summer, all the new younger kids took the Red Car to Hermosa Beach and hung out by the pier near that big hotel. The retired older men you knew continued to meet at Carmel's drugstore up on west Highland. They never went back to Murdoch's, even when it opened with the new owner. And sadly, most of them are dead now.

"Red Owens is still here in Manhattan Beach acting like God's gift to law enforcement. But it hasn't been so easy for him. Dolores finally got fed up and left him and Russ Junior and Manhattan Beach. I think she moved up north somewhere. Maybe Oakland or San Francisco. Russ Jr. was 4-F and spent the whole war working at the Douglas plant in Long Beach. He's married now, lives in Long Beach and doesn't come back here so Red never sees him or the grandchildren. And Hazel Carter moved away, too; close to her sister in Santa Monica. Did you know, George, Dolores was Miss Manhattan Beach in 1920 and Hazel was runner-up?" Helen said."

"No, Mom, I never knew that. Well, Hazel was a very nice lady, sure put up with a lot with Larry and was really a great help at the drugstore. But what happened to Big Al? I used to send some letters but when I never heard from him, I stopped writing. I wonder if he ever got them?" George said.

"To tell the truth, son, from what I heard, Big Al never got over what happened to you. He lost you as a friend and someone to talk to. I also heard he was very angry at Lefty: thought Red Owens, the police detective or whatever he was at the time, a bad apple, and that it was Red's constant obsession and talking about you in public, even after the grand jury decision, was what killed Lefty's business...not you. And Lefty just never stood up, went to the Chief of Police, or made Red Owens stop. But I always wondered, too, why Lefty did nothing. But then, what could Lefty do anyway? As for your letters to Big Al, I never did hear anything about them. And Big Al died about four years ago."

"That sure explains why I never heard from him. Okay, enough is enough, Mom, except I do want to say how hard it was when I got the news that Carolyn Hodge drowned."

"Yes, it was a terrible tragedy, son. There were very bad rip tides that day. And she was such a great swimmer and knew the ocean so well. She never should have gone in by herself. It just made no sense that she would take such a risk. None of us could figure out what possessed her to do such a crazy thing. I took it hard too, son, as Carolyn always came by, and we shared the letters you wrote to me, and the ones you wrote to her. She was like a daughter."

Changing the subject quickly, George said, "Mom, tomorrow I'm going to Hermosa Beach, down near the pier, to Miller's Clothing Store, if it's still there, to get some clothes. Can't wear a uniform anymore and none of the few things left here fit me. I've got plenty of mustering-out pay that will get me started. Then I can look for a job."

"Miller's is still there. You're right, you've grown even taller and those old clothes won't fit."

"Not taller, Mom, just huskier and stronger. You don't walk over half of North Africa and Europe and not get huskier!" George said laughing.

George got off the Red Car below the Strand at 28th Street, climbed the stairs to the Strand and walked slowly up 28th Street to Ocean Drive… bent slightly forward, and in the same rhythmic, plodding pace of an infantryman. Suddenly, the same uneasy feeling he'd had so many times in combat overcame him. He stopped. George became cautious, alert. He crouched down, looked around. Seeing nothing, George started to laugh, he reminded himself the war was over, and he was at home, safe and sound.

He'd bought some work pants, shirts and shoes. He figured he could still use his army short jacket when it was cool and take the Sergeant's stripes off. When he turned left on Ocean Drive, George spotted a police squad car parked in front of his mother's house. Maybe his uneasy feeling was right he thought.

As George reached the house, Red Owens got out of the police car, planted his feet wide apart, pushed his sports coat back and moved his hand on to his belt near his service revolver. It was all George could do not to burst out laughing.

"Well, if it isn't our star athlete, war hero come home and back to civilian control," Red snarled sarcastically.

George didn't react to Red's sarcasm but said simply, "Hello, Red, how's everything?"

"I'll tell you how it is hot shot. Our file on the murder at the former Murdoch drugstore was never closed, and I'm going to nail your ass for it yet. We'll be bringing you in for one of those new polygraph tests, "lie detector test" to you, Fisher. I've already got the Los Angeles Police

Department expert lined up to administer the test. So don't try to leave town, understand? Like trying to get back into the army and be off to some cushy overseas assignment. This time I'll get you, understand, Fisher?"

"Anything you say, Red. I'll be right here, or out looking for a job."

"You can forget the job bit, Mr. Star Athlete. I've spread the word, and no one will want to hire you. We've got long memories here, Fisher. I'll be in touch." And with that, Red got back in the police car, laughed and drove off.

George told his mother about his encounter with Red when she came home from work. He said it was hard to believe that Red Owens was still ruining his life by conducting a 'hate and George-Fisher-is-guilty, campaign.' Helen said not to worry, she knew her son had told the truth about what happened on that Sunday so long ago: he was not in the drugstore when the horrible crime happened, and no lie test, or whatever it's called, was going to change the truth be told. Maybe all Red Owens had left in life, Helen said, was his hate, hate that had cost him, dearly.

After a couple of weeks, Red's statement about no one hiring George Fisher came true. No matter where he tried, no one wanted him: Moore's Market; the Bakery; E-Z Electric; Manhattan Hardware; Builder's Material Co; and both the gas stations. The new owner of Murdoch's Drugstore threatened to throw George out the door until he thought better of it. No job for George Fisher, was the rule, especially with the Red Owens anti-Fisher campaign in full force and so many vets looking for work. Though Manhattan Beach grew some during the war, it was still a small town of less than seven thousand people with a very tight-knit, small business community. And no one could afford to do anything that would lose customers. Everyone remembered too well what had happened to Lefty Murdoch and his business.

George was able to locate Rocco Ronning, one of the members of the Morning Sports Club and the Ace of Clubs and went to see him. With Rocco's guidance, the balance of his mustering-out pay, a GI Bill small business loan, and some modest help from his mother, George bought a half interest in the bait shack out on the pier and went into business for himself. Red Owens tried to block the deal, but pressure from the American Legion and the threat of a lawsuit stopped him. What Red didn't know was that George got a long-term extension on the pier bait shack lease site from the city, with a future option to put in a soda fountain-lunch-counter. George felt maybe things were going to change. Or so he hoped.

But early in January of '46, George Fisher, aka, "Giant Malt George," was served a subpoena by the Los Angeles County District Attorney's office to appear at the superior court in Los Angeles for a polygraph test. George learned he didn't have to agree to take the test but felt taking it was the only way to put an end to the Red Owens hate campaign. So, George said yes to the test and took one of the new Pacific Electric buses into Los Angeles. A Lt. Purdy from the L.A.P.D. conducted the test; questions came from the Manhattan Beach Police Department except for the usual introductory ones about name, age, date of birth, address, etc.

Several weeks later the report came in. One copy went to the chief of police in Manhattan Beach, one to the lawyer George got pro-bono through the American Legion and one to the Superior Court in Los Angeles. The results were unequivocal: "The subject George Fisher has spoken truthfully about his activities and whereabouts on November 27, 1939. There is no indication George Fisher was in any way, or in any manner, involved in or connected with the death of one Larry Carter at the Murdoch Drugstore on said day." The "Daily Breeze" covered the report briefly.

George thought this was finally the end of everything. But Red Owens held another press conference where he announced his intention to keep up his investigation. "George Fisher did it and I'm going to prove it," were his final words. The "Daily Breeze" editorialized that there must be something to Red Owens story, otherwise, a veteran detective like Red wouldn't still be so adamant about his continued investigation of George Fisher.

So, the whispers, dirty looks and shunning of George Fisher began all over again. George, now a little depressed, usually stayed away from everyone, or just worked extra hours at the bait shop where the customers were mainly fishermen from places other than Manhattan Beach. George began to wonder if he should go back into the army. Maybe Major Pierce was right about, 'If things don't work out, you can re-enlist.'

Helen Fisher opened the back door, walked into the kitchen, and found George sitting at the small kitchen table. "How did it go today, dear?" she asked.

"Mom, there aren't so many guys fishing off the pier anymore. Lots have some money now, so they go down to Redondo Beach and take one of the all-day or half-day boats out to fish. And the pier crowds always did drop off anyway after school began," George answered.

"Have you thought about moving away from all the bad feelings here, son?"

"Yes, I thought about it. But I've got to face facts, Mom. Red Owens is not going to drive me away. After all the combat stuff in the war: landings, infantry-supported tank battles, artillery bombardments, patrols and hand-to-hand killing. Well, Red Owens's trying to blame me for a killing I didn't do is simply BS. It's like Red is trying to goad me into doing something. Doing something that would get me into real trouble. Red is a real bad guy, Mom. I used to see guys like him in the army. They'd scheme so hard to get everything their way they'd do anything, and I mean, anything, Mom. So maybe I don't want to bother with a guy like Red Owens. But if I don't, if I don't understand him and see what he's up to, I won't survive. And if I turned tail and ran, what would I do? How would I have any self-respect, and what would all the men I knew who faced death every day and didn't make it home think of a guy like Red Owens and his petty life? But heck, all I know is how to work at a soda fountain, sell bait and fishing gear, talk fishing and sports or be an NCO in a rifle company."

Sensing her son's mood, Helen changed the subject quickly. She said, "One of the ladies at work brought in a scrapbook today. It reminded me of something. It was in the early spring of '43 just before Carolyn drowned when she came by and left a box for you. She said it was some souvenirs, and I put it in the old hutch in the living room and clean forgot about it. I'll get it for you."

Helen got the box. It was tied with twine and on the top was written, "George, Love, Carolyn." George took the box, stood up and went back to his room. He thought of Carolyn who'd drowned just after his division landed in Tunisia. After he got the news, he volunteered for any kind of high-risk patrol and fought his way through North Africa, Sicily, France and Germany. George thought how strange life was: Carolyn dies right here in the surf near where we went to the beach on dates; and me, from '43 to '45 in virtually constant combat, I never got anything more than a few minor wounds and Purple Hearts.

George sat down on the bed, opened the souvenir box and emptied the contents on the bed in front of him. It held some newspaper clippings about the Sea Hawks winning the Bay League and southern division CIF championship in basketball, his great last-second shot, and a picture of the entire team. There was his graduation ring the school gave him and that he gave to Carolyn, some ticket stubs from the Venice Ballroom, a senior prom program and a picture of Carolyn in her sensational swim suit standing by the Curries Mile High 5 cent Cone store near the pier in Hermosa Beach. George remembered that day: how great the surfing and swimming was, and how Carolyn had kissed him that night when he walked her home.

George almost missed the small white envelope stuck into a fold of the carton flaps at the bottom of the box. He pulled it loose, opened it and found a letter folded into a neat square inside. He took it out and opened it. It was handwritten:

My Dear George,

I came home early that Sunday from Palos Verdes, got off the Red Car at the pier and went to the drugstore in hopes of seeing you. Mr. Carter let me in and said you were in the back. I looked at the Evening in Paris display near the door. Mr. Carter grabbed me from behind and the display got tipped over.

He tried to put his hands all over me. I got loose and ran fast to the back of the store; I called for you. Mr. Carter chased me. I knocked over the ball display in the big metal rack. Mr. Carter tripped on it and crashed into the raised soda fountain floor. I thought he was just stunned, like a football player with the wind knocked out of him. I ran to the front door and unlocked it with the key that was already in the lock. I never took any money. I was so scared everyone would blame me because "pretty girls attract men."

Forgive me for not speaking up. I did take the key and locked the door so Mr. Carter could not chase me again. I threw the key away. Please, please forgive me. I also kept silent, so poor Hazel Carter would not be shamed.

I love you. I pray you'll come home safely. Please understand. I'm so ashamed. I've failed you.

All my love,
Carolyn

George read the note over and over. For a tough, combat infantryman tears poured freely down his face. Poor Carolyn, he said to himself. Sure, he knew why she kept quiet. Who would believe it was an accident, not a murder, but an accident caused by "Clutching Carter" himself? The guy with the reputation that everyone, even Hazel Carter, knew about. And Red Owens would just say that George Fisher...the "Hot shot, the Star Athlete"...put Carolyn up to telling her story to cover up for her boyfriend. And then the whole thing would get even worse with Red Owens attacking Carolyn's story, reputation and her "real" relationship to Giant Malt George.

And now, what's the use, George thought as he folded the note, put it in the envelope and placed it and all the memories back in the small souvenir box. And he asked out loud, "Who would believe what really happened? Who cares? And who is going to ask how Red Owens knew exactly how much money was in that 'empty' cash register on that Monday morning so long ago? Or if Red Owens guessed Larry Carter might have let someone else in the drugstore that morning? Or if Red Owens never wanted to really solve anything? Only wanted his hate, and to "prove" George Fisher did it?"

Giant Malt George knew the answers to his questions. He stood up and decided to walk down to the pier to see if the fish were biting.

Fragment: Another Beginning 1941-1949

Commentary

In nearly every recorded life-saga, events seem to happen in what looks like occurrences happen in a continuous, casual sequence; this is often done to disguise what is really going on before it becomes obvious that there is more at stake than the reader knows so far. The writer does this on purpose to make the reader believe in a conclusion that seems to predict how the story will end. However, suddenly the reader is surprised by twists in the plot that reveal, as the story continues, that the prior anticipated end was viewed either casually or fortuitously; however, then astute readers realize very little in life occurs instantly because there is always the action of *Time* to reckon with and so clues of unexpected, or upcoming crises and/ or disasters, are still hidden. Recognize as well, it is evident the narrator describes life carelessly from *memory* which may color remembrances so that the events narrated were selected with a purpose by the writer and only *fragments* of reality, perhaps, that fit *Events* are related.

"Note, Life is also Time:
And Time is most often a Series of Fragments"

P. Kaufman, 1991

For example, *looking way back I thought 7th grade in 1941 had hopes of stability, I was wrong.* First, we moved back to California to our new home in an isolated area the locals called, "PV", for Palos Verdes. That move happened just after Labor Day 1940, which is when school started.

31

Later, in the summer of 1941, we move again, it was back east for 8th grade and my seeing friends, once again in Pennsylvania, where my grandmother lives. On December 7, 1941, when WW II started out in the Pacific Ocean at an island called Hawaii, I was in Greensburg, which was very far from us in Pennsylvania. Soon the older guys who were getting ready for/or were in High School, talked about which branch of the Service to volunteer for, especially since there were lots of veterans from WW I living on both sides of my grandmother's house as well as all over town; they talked to us about war and what it meant.

But that changed again soon, too, when we packed up once more and moved back to *PV* to start High School in September of 1942 at Redondo Union High School. I liked how things were going until the night my mother sent me out on my bicycle to ride up to the Plaza to get her cigarettes at the drug store, which was to stay open until I got there. It didn't. I started home; it was very dark and quiet because of Black-Outs and no traffic or street lights like I was used to in Pennsylvania. We had military patrols too, that I knew nothing about; I could not see anything, but off I went, full speed, down the steep hill from the drug store on my bike on the way home.

I met the army patrol jeep somewhere around the bottom of the hill, head-on. The next thing I remember is first aid at the gas station, and someone saying, 'His bleeding is stopping.' that was not true...until the surgeon at the hospital in Torrance sewed up my left leg, just below the knee. It was the surgeon's last night before Army duty. I was lucky, everyone said, because he was so good; but I still carry the scars today, and when it's damp and cold my leg hurts. The two soldiers from the patrol came to the hospital to see me; I often wondered if they survived the war. Their unit was part of the anti-air-craft battery in the open fields between Hollywood Riviera, PV and Redondo Beach. They were very kind to me but felt so badly because they had not seen nor heard me coming...me too. I felt badly too because maybe I also might have seen them.

The High School in Redondo Beach, 1942-1943 had top athletic teams in football, basketball and baseball. I had stability all the way through the school year and half of next year when disaster struck again with the sale of our home in Palos Verdes in 1943; when, the decision to return to Pennsylvania was made just before Christmas. My sister and I moved back to Greensburg for the second half of the current High School year

1943-1944 right at Christmas time. When summer came, it was back to California again but now we were living in Manhattan Beach in a small two-story bungalow, near the center of town off the road that leads to the City Pier. Then, a really bad thing suddenly happened…my father, who lived in near-by Hermosa Beach, appeared and insisted that my sister, who had only one year left in High School, and I had to go to other schools to finish and graduate from what Dad considered, 'college preparatory schools.'"

Bad Idea, 1945

"The idea was bad since it meant, for the first time, my sister and I were separated; we were great friends and depended on each other quite a bit: caring, sharing and working out our problems, disappointments and helping each other with homework and, for me, getting used to a new kind of school culture. In isolated *PV*, we especially needed one another…at one terrible time I helped drive off some man who had broken into the house and tried to attack my sister…little me, with my air gun as a club, but it was the State police who came, caught him hiding in one of the showers, and we were both saved.

"My father picked out schools: mine, was in Colorado, my sister's in Pasadena. As it turned out, she could not get the necessary classes to graduate, they were all filled; so, she went back to Pennsylvania to live with our grandmother for the Senior High School year; I went to a school called, Valley High, in Colorado. My sister wrote to me every week and made it plain how much she missed me; she hoped I would be able to come to her graduation.

"Recalling classes in Colorado, I remember more Algebra, Latin, United States and Pennsylvania History, General Science, Biology, English and Grammar. At each of the high schools I attended, I was asked to take notes on the ability of a teacher's presentation. It was a strange request but the only thing I noted in my notes, under the quality of the lessons was the observation: my favorite class was Biology…guess which part?

"Female anatomy?"

"Of course!"

Valley High School, 1944-1946

Commentary

Because of the train schedules during the war, I arrived a day early in Colorado Springs, was met at the station and driven to the new school south of the city. I was assigned a room, unpacked the new clothes I had to have for Sunday dinner and chapel and waited for tomorrow when everyone arrived; class schedules were given out and I had a chance to become acquainted with my new surroundings. Not having my sister with me and being all alone without my grandmother also made me apprehensive. I didn't sleep very much for several nights.

The class schedule included: 3rd year Latin, US History, Chemistry, advanced Algebra, English and a class on Saturday in Public speaking. Some of the guys I met were unfriendly maybe because I was a 'new guy' and perhaps a threat to the established pecking order. There were a couple of exceptions to unfriendliness: a guy, John, from Omaha, Nebraska and Jim, a local guy from Colorado Springs.

I had a letter waiting for me at the school post office from my sister; she missed me so much; wanted to know what the school was like and my class schedule. She sent me her schedule and told me Grandmother missed me very much, too. She said she would graduate on schedule and hoped I would be there for the ceremony.

The School had strange names for the school years: I was in the Fifth Form and not Junior year. In third year Latin there were only two of us; that meant it was tough. Football started and one of my roommates was from Fort Worth who played half back and carried a comb in his uniform football pants to comb his hair (he did regularly). He smoked secretly in the small bedroom closet behind the curtain, and even cheated at poker. He figured out right away I knew what he was doing; I was smart, never said anything.

Time began to pass quickly, *once I passed beyond being watched all the time as a problem because of all my moves and different schools.* Then, I earned the privilege of taking the school bus into Colorado Springs after the public speaking class on Saturday, so I could get my allowance from the school Savings Account in my name, go to a movie, get chocolate covered mints at Stern's and be by myself; no money could be kept in a school bedroom.

Another letter came from my sister and she asked me if I was coming to Pennsylvania for Christmas vacation? A quick check with the school accountant answered that: *no way.* I was going back to California; the tickets were already purchased to go to San Bernardino where Mom would meet me. Later, she would drive us to the small house in Palm Springs where she lived, and we took walks to a café to eat since Mom did not like to cook and wanted time alone with me to talk about my quitting school in Colorado and going to High School in Palm Springs or Redondo Beach. At the end of one week in San Bernardino, we drove to Manhattan Beach.

When we got there, I stored my stuff in the downstairs bedroom, then Mom and I walked up to Hal's for a sandwich and she asked me to think about quitting Colorado and moving back to California. That made some sense until *I saw a familiar Bank of America envelope* at the table in the Morningside Drive house. I looked at it and began thinking about changing High Schools again. But, I really didn't see how I could move with the demand for room space for all of us either in Palm Springs or Manhattan Beach; but Mom was determined that I quit Colorado and move; I thought about the letter from B of A and the check in it for $150 for Christmas vacation expenses for me.

The next night Mom said she was going out for a while to meet an old friend, have a drink and would be back in an hour or so. After mom left I thought more about my coming to Southern California for Christmas, where I was now, and the $150 check from B of A, which was no longer in the envelope. I saw that my presence was worth money, that it is now going to Valley School, not to Mom; that I was *worth* money and who got it made a difference and it was worth maneuvering to get it; after what happened next. I stayed in Colorado until graduation; and, of course, my sister, and her money stayed in Pennsylvania until her graduation and she went on to Pomona College in California.

Driving Under the Influence of Liquor

I recall, Mom said she was going out to see some friends and would be back in about an hour or so. But Mom did not return until much, much later so I fell asleep and awakened around 8: 30 in the morning. It turned out Mom was detained by the police when she was stopped coming out of Hal's and tried *to drive under the influence.* An officer was supposed to let me know she would be along in the morning...it never happened.

So, I'd spent the evening *alone* trying to piece together what really went wrong after our home in *PV* was sold; how Mom messed up her financial future, and ours in college, by never having a real home again and raiding trusts. It took me many years to try to fit the pieces of the puzzle together, plus making assumptions and guesses about whether my conclusions were correct or not.

Here's what I believe happened: *(A) Mom and her boyfriend became convinced that when PV was sold, all three trustees would get equal shares. Since Mom had been successful in getting B of A to always give her extra money from the kids' Trusts, money for their extra expenses, really Mom's ;she, not her boyfriend, would get a full share from the house sale, but also extra from the kids' trusts for years as in the past; (B)however, along came the kids' Dad with his unexpected private school idea; I end up in expensive Colorado for my last two High School years and then it's on to college for more costly years; my sister is in college where her money continues to go after High School graduation, in 1945, and now for another three full college years; (C), so much, for Mom's and her boyfriend's plot, scheme to loot the kids' trust funds by getting B of A to increase money to Mom.*

Carmel Valley 1945-1946

Never out of ideas, I learned Mother came up with a new plot; she found a home for sale on a big lot in Carmel Valley; near another of her favorite spots, Carmel. Now it's back to B of A to set up the same sort of situation as PV; all three of us would buy the property, share in the purchase, and, of course, all subsequent carrying costs. The Trust Officer in charge of the trusts at B of A turned it down immediately. So, Mom decided to develop a sub scheme; she wanted our grandmother to sell her two small homes in Pennsylvania, after my sister completes high school, in 1945, and both of them can continue the move cycle and come to California and Carmel and the new home, which Mom says she already owns, and everyone can share in the operating costs. The idea died four times: first, at B of A, with

Grandmother, followed by we kids, and finally by default with Mom's boyfriend who never had a cent anyway. My view of Mom's latest attempt was simple: boyfriends had lived off us for years, so his *share had to come from the famous kid's trust funds as it had for the last ten years.*

Last College Semester, 1949

Brief Summary: at the end of my last college semester, I borrowed immediate money to finish my final semester in 1950 before I began my job with Chase bank in New York and Service in the USAF in the Korean War. Because of the past events however: private school costs, endless train trips and robbing trust funds for daily costs for everyone, including B of A with its final trust fees...these realities made sure we kid's trust funds were virtually bankrupt. Also there was no way Grandmother would ever have enough money, or would she ever leave her home in Pennsylvania; and my sister was never ever going to voluntarily join another, PV type program that would complete the bankrupting of her trust fund when she still had to pay to finish her college years and her early marriage still happening. (But she had avoided Dad's private school idea and perhaps any other future milking of trust fund thoughts). However, now a popular idea of how to make ends meet, Carmel Valley, with kids and Grandmother the victims was tested. By then however, we were older, really had no funds anyway, and maybe wiser.

Fragment – The Red Ass

Tales of Self-Deception

Note:
The red ass is a popular expression
in southern states
in the '40s which means to
be very angry, to be livid or
even to be pissed off.
Introduction

Basic Theory

"It was a time in the 70s when the future was success, pure success...
endless success; part of the goal was to "Get More"; all one had
to do was to reach out and grab it...be bold and grab it. It was a
theory: not a race of Hares vs. Tortoises, but like an atmosphere in
which Greed was spreading like an infection, carried on the wind,
and the content was: Total Independence; High Risk; High Debt
creation for leverage and High Spending; always, High Spending
with Low Responsibility; Only Hares survive; Tortoises perish.
"The daily Mantra was, Who Dares Win, just hit the world with a Basic
Agenda that debt was built on credit, always someone else's credit, for
getting the gold from the real estate boom. One trick was to build two
homes simultaneously which created the happy opportunity of erasing
the debt amassed in the building of the first structure by borrowing from

Human Nature

the construction loan for the second structure and applying it to existing prior debt. The reasoning was both a question of timing and finding additional credit sources from family, especially friends and significant others to hold off credit card, open account and debt collection pests."

Reality

Absent from this cheerful, brilliant theory, of course, are certain realities: funding limits, lenders tracking expenditures from a construction loan to its proper, correct site for the application of the funds; market forces such as: interest rate changes…especially on construction loans (ask the Carter Administration about rates in excess of 12% for High Risk construction loans), status of the general economy, public buying confidence for large ticket items like homes, automobiles and the growing absence of critical discretionary spending.

Inconvenience #1 to Basic Theory

"The Basic Theory suffered a significant betrayal when banks; lumber yards; appliance distributors; paint; tile; custom window suppliers… and all other major sources of building materials demanded up-front cash so that the open account wonderland ended. Another blow was to artistic perfectionism which made building a home for profit, like a businessman would do, impossible as one could no longer change, tear out or redo work product that offended artistic sensitivity, temperament etc. This had the effect of impacting the obsession that building a residence was a personal achievement and any cost add-on needed could be easily handled by increasing the home sales price; also, any over runs of construction loan amounts by adjustments, with a simple request to change them, as in the past, with the bank. Of course, the cost of perfectionism is an integral part of Basic Theory as well personality, and the Agenda of spending, spending. No amount of hostility was effective in modifying cash now, to more credit now. Another costly blow was the new restrictions that ended referral fees for steering buyers to closing cost specialists as well as furniture, appliance, landscape, etc. retail outlets."

Reality Response to Inconvenience #1 to Basic Theory

By 1982, Theory faced more realities: sales were slowing and the continued decline in the economy hit the rate of new home sales which were in competition with sales of existing housing which had the advantage of being able to lower the asking price. The passage of property tax laws also played a part, too, since Real Property taxation for a current sale was often, by law, set at some percent of the transaction amount. So, the increase of a house price to satisfy various cost increases in the building process such as higher interest rates on High Risk construction loans, all acted to increase the home price to recover those total construction costs. And, therefore, Real Property taxes at one percent of the transaction amount, for example, on a home selling at @$250,000, the first year the Real Property tax is $2,500 or $208.33 dollars per month which is added to the monthly payment to retire, eventually, a fully amortized mortgage; there were no interest only payment type loans anymore.

Inconvenience #2 to Basic Theory

"Ok, the 1982 recession spelled a suspension of the Basic Theory for a short time in the housing boom and sure-fire Bankruptcy avoidance which might be a bi-product of out of phase, at this time, of High Risk, High Debt creation, High Spending and construction loan manipulation. Many dedicated theorists were forced to switch construction skills, expensive skills, to home repair, maintenance and modifications. This was a natural site for expensive taste artistic flare builders who, for the most part, always used snob appeal to market to high salary home owners who, because of their money, always demand a first class, ok, extravagant builder. Now the theorist builder can re-do a kitchen for the wife; a computer-room, library for the husband; or even add an additional room to the home; so, because I have an obsession about certain product manufacturers, I can easily persuade this high income buyer, he/she, will be happier following my superior skills, independence and advice; just sell the idea 'you are what you buy and your home should reflect your personality.'"

Reality Response to Inconvenience #2 to Basic Theory

Rule number one for modification construction means meeting the schedule of the owner who is putting up the money and dictates how the money is spent. This is critical because modification is not a brand-new home where the completion schedule can be often at the whim of the creative artist/ builder. Maybe what this boils down to is can the Theorist kind of guy work well for others? Hint, how about the employment record in prior year? Do we have other clues about the success of working for others? Ok, what happens when a perfectionist insists on High, Total Independence for a specific product(s) and it does not arrive in time to meet the completion schedule agreed upon by the home owner; and our personal achievement, creative builder...is fired...what is the long-term penalty?

Inconvenience #3 to Basic Theory

"Current events by 1984 suggest the new house construction market is not at this time the place for an under-capitalized, small entrepreneur builder who is often forced to wait it out and watch the interest cost on the current construction loan bankrupt him alive before the house sells. The home usually sells at a foreclosure price far less than the cost to build it. Such an event is further aggravated by the square foot price of full value Homeowners Insurance to rebuild the entire structure. This is critical as the cost of full value Homeowners insurance on a-per-square foot premium basis for complete reconstruction generates a total cost at a level higher than the house is worth on the open market. Full value Homeowners insurance is mandatory to obtain a take-out-loan from a new lender to cover the take-out loan risk in the event of total loss. The net impact means the small builder must obtain employment as a Manager for a premium, big boy builder. Personal independence, as a result, is out the window. Also, in trouble is the demand for Total Independence…a primary item in the Basic Theory of how to cash in on the housing boom; how much trouble?"

Reality Response to Inconvenience #3 to Basic Theory

The theorist is unhappy; angry; pissed off; going to work every day at a place which he believes he can run better than it is being run now; the top guy however, knows what the theorist is thinking, in so many words, and so again, the theorist who becomes disaffected, is fired; but he's still convinced he was right and one day he will prove it.

"…It's money that I love,
it's money that I love…"

It's Money That I Love, Randy Newman, 1979

Inconvenience #4 to Basic Theory

"Fighting back, even though it's another Manager position at the last big builder out-fit still operating in my area, they hire me. Since family expenses are up, the idea is to take the job, keep quiet and wait for housing to come back; also for the good old days of financial support, like during school, the first of the building boom when the market was hot and renewed family connections with plenty of money would be there in 'my hour of need'…and like the Business outfits I bought so much from in the past and business credit was the rule which saw me through the early years of the mess until the last two years of Hell set in, and friends to tap disappeared; but it didn't work out that way… everyone became Hostile and hounded ruthlessly to pay up. Despite the Basic Theory, which is the way to success, hanging on to the new job is critical despite an attitude and reputation for being disaffected which is well known in the building trade; it's a big difference when you're the 'boss' vs. being an employee; and both sides have never forgotten it."

Reality Inconvenience Response #4 to Basic Theory

When the stubborn anger factor begins, re-enters the picture...it soon matures into more than Hostility, it becomes Animosity, which when uncontrolled causes the burning of bridges with the supporters you ignored, and with whom you have strongly disagreed, especially their advice. Worse still, you may come to believe all these people from your past are sitting on piles of cash and credit which they can use to come to your aid. Despite the fact you are the author of your predicament and not a victim of it as you have always maintained. Moreover, Theorists have become what in British English they call a 'Wide Boys'...people who are shady characters, a Sharpies; results, firings.

"See the dark night has come down on us
the world is livin' in its dreams...
but now we know that we can wake up..."

The Ark, Gerry Raffery, 1978

Inconvenience #5 to Basic Theory

"The Basic Theory, of course, includes Spending, always
High Spending, there is plenty of room to convert the credit
instruments of others to your use which, once prosperity returns,
such debts can easily be retired...a rising tide lifts all boats."

Reality Inconvenience Response #5 to Basic Theory

Except, the owners of such credit instruments, (cards), may find this is not the time of forgiveness since the loss of their personal property may have caused foreclosure and the subsequent permanent loss of capital assets; so, there is no consent to satisfy debts of others for which they are not responsible.

Inconvenience #6 to Basic Theory

"By 1985, the housing market is in recovery but old scores come
up for settlement; the use of other's credit instruments; arrogant
attitudes about who is boss emerge; hostility and anger at the loss
of money because of past practices and the belief that building a
home is a for profit business, not just an form; except in rare cases
where snob appeal is part of the project and cost is not a factor."

Reality Inconvenience Response #6 to Basic Theory

The events in these tales illustrate the causes of Theorist:
terminations; however, which one is the deadliest? Is it important?

'We can accept a person only to the extent that we are not
threatened by him; if a person is hostile toward me, and I can
see nothing in him at the moment except hostility, I am quite
sure that I will react in a defensive way to the hostility.'

As quoted in Motivation and Personality; Second Edition, 1970
Abraham H. Maslow

Basic Theory Revisited and Justified

"The fact is you are what you do...not this predetermined good guy/
bad guy crap that you do what you are. 'For example, the Greeks
believe (what did they know so many centuries ago?) that there is
some sort of Gods called The Fates who assign your life to you when
you are born; you will be just what The Fates determine for you.
Look them up: there are three Fates, sisters, Clotho, Lechesis and
Atropos. Who decide your destiny either evil or good; depending
whatever your Lot is, that is what you will be...you can't change it'?
"Well, that stuff is bunk, to hit it big and prove to everyone what is right
that the only thing screwing up success is people, especially family, that
sit on plenty of money and is too cheap to give others their share. So,
you've got expensive tastes; need money for everything: the best tools,

cameras, cars, pick-up-trucks...you name it; you are what you buy: Be
a taker, want the best; what you earn is yours, if you have a significant
other, or family member, that has a job, money, property, you name
it, then part of that is yours, too, to help you hit the big times. So you
encounter a down real estate market in 1982 and afterwards; so, later you
had Bankruptcies. You'll come back...all you need, NOW, is significant
money, not chicken feed or small amounts spread out over time...you
want gifts...not loans: not Micro amounts but Macro amounts, up front.
With the right money backing you, you're a cinch to be rich and famous."

Basic Reality Revisited

A Basic Theory based on self-deception as to the nature of risk in
the real world and meeting consequences by: demanding continuous,
endless gifts of money to overcome your mistakes; counting yourself
a victim; meeting your repetitious, self-caused set-backs, in later
life, by blaming others; having hostility, anger, being pissed-off,
and getting The Red Ass only means Disaster; do The Fate's
Lots in fact, represent ultimate character and personality?
With Sorrow and Despair, we must conclude: that major philosophical
miscalculations, stubbornness and failure to modify when realities, in
parallel with new events that impact life...compared to those realities
that existed at the time the fundamental obsessions of: Big Risks; Big
Debts; Big Spending; Big Income; Big Credit Instruments; Total Job
Control; and Low Responsibility; etc., were first established as the
essential Basic Elements necessary for a prosperous, successful life, do
indeed, mean: The Fates cannot be turned: You do what you are.
But unlike The Fates, there are religious condemned obsessions: Vanity,
Greed, Pride and Delight...in addition to ultimate Death, that are
represented on a remarkable town hall astronomical clock in the Old
Town Square in Prague. Statues made to resemble those traits are
displayed as twin sets: Vanity and Greed, and Delight and Death on
opposite sides of the clock face. Both sets rotate every hour: left and
right respectively. The clock reflects as well: the current time in two 12-
hour increments; each hour has specific Latin words describing life-time

personality element…as at birth, youth, afternoon, twilight, etc.; and finally, there are, permanent statues of the 12 Apostles. Unlike The Fates, however, the Moral lecture on the clock avoids the permanent, fatalistic finality of Vanity; Pride; Greed…Avarice; and Delight; to Covet… both the object desired and the person who has it: all of which are changeable before Death; it is doubtful, however, the medieval morality lecture is understood by the throngs that for hundreds of years come to view the clock and whether any behavior is modified. Nota bene, if belief in self is the only existent thing, you do what you are.

End Notes

"Two are just; but are not listened to there;
Pride, Envy, and Avarice are the three sparks
which set the hearts of all on fire."
"… tell me where they are, and give me to know them:
for great desire urges me to learn whether
Heaven soothes or Hell empoisons them."
"They are amongst the blackest
spirits; a different crime weighs them down-
wards to the bottom, shouldst thou descend
so far, thou mayest see them."

Dante, The Inferno, Canto VI, 1909, Emphasis added

"It may easily pass that a vain man may become proud and imagine himself pleasing to all when he is in reality a universal nuisance."

Spinoza, Ethics, 1707, London, English edition, Emphasis added

Repetition

Self-deception permeates
An empty theory
Like an incessant wind
That escapes reality through
Repetition
Repetition
And still more repetition,
Of what needs no repetition.

Daily concocted
Excuses for rationalizations
Augment an already
Perfected façade of Pride
And Avarice,
Rooted in self-deception,
Like an insistent vacuum
Sucking us dry.

But the wind continues
Reversing
Spiraling
Questioning excuses for
Repetition
Repetition
And still more repetition.
Of what needs no repetition.

While such daily repetition
Procures ephemeral Perfection,
For a verity,
Rooted in sterile self-deception
While Covetousness
Still creates victims for
That insistent vacuum
Sucking us dry.

P. Kaufman

Fragment: 1983

'.....you better let somebody love you...
Before it's too late...'
Desperado, (D. Henley/G. Frey) 1976

Commentary

When finally out of the Air Force forever in 1962, Percy encounters Lynne and Victoria again at my new job site in California; among other things, they are wrestling with a phrase of being *'good for'* someone else; he felt both were searching for a workable feeling, like love, or a key phrase that both could use; frequently; however, it seemed in the California culture, with its speed of change, that being *'good for'* another person, is slippery, because the very elusiveness of being good, is indeed, an obsession often more in the mind than anywhere else. Still, I had special hope for Victoria; she must continue to mature and have confidence to be an Assistant.

Percy continues thinking about his job with the new group of women, two of whom are Lynne and Victoria, with Victoria, still in the background, but a promising background. Moreover, he learns both are quite socially active and prominent. Since both frequently hire me to teach them about financial responsibility, especially Victoria, I drive *their* cars and listen to their conversations which are: like two gals out to shopping, an entire family on the way to the beach, a single person to church, or just a romantic couple who say little but hug and kiss passionately during the entire trip.

As it usually works out, Percy, waits for his customers to begin the conversation; he gets satisfaction in learning, that their current trip is also only part of a reality which makes him a key part of the total project, not merely taking them from place A to place B.

Bit by bit, he begins to decipher that part of his job is part of completing tasks for others, especially Victoria, to help achieve her current goal; so, an important part of *their* talk, is for him to realize his objective of getting an assistant is now complete…it's Lynne. However, he does understand that driving them, listening to their genuine concerns, maybe it's also a *Control* for me, too, since I'm learning from others what it is to achieve major important goals; not just a minor fragment like in everyday life; such as going to the market, but real shopping is at Neiman Marcus, inside changing room with Lynne for *lingerie*, afternoon.

So, frequently, I remind Lynne about driving a person who shares; how rewarding it is to have a reliable driver to get an opinion, and not having to drive on her own, or look for a random opinion, which gives her usually an hour of uninterrupted time to think and share private, even very personal, intimate stuff, like about which panties to buy or an "after shopping massage and exercise".

All this made me recall how long ago, I planned weekends with Jesse's friend Rita during High School in Santa Barbara to save money, so I could pay for lunch in the school cafeteria, then by hearing about her in the park, especially her favorite life cycle and favorite habit: remove any *Sameness* for *Newness and the obsessive cycle it creates*. I recognized a missing, critical absent term in her cycle which I called *Satisfaction*. Lynne agreed, which was to some extent, that her new career is, indeed, a step to seeing satisfaction as part, a larger piece, in her bigger, major undertaking of continuing the sameness/ newness part of her cycle but with the addition *of another changing room and real satisfaction.*

Changing Room

As usual, my *'in control' highly social customer, Lynne,* is always a frequent and expected user of Percy's Financial and Other Services Disciplines; unlike Victoria, Lynn said, "I always restrict shopping…so far very successfully." Especially my trips for clothing: all kinds including, swim wear, daily dresses, evening gowns, and eventually, of course, even some lingerie which

I try on in the changing rooms at *Neiman Marcus* with all their facilities. The system includes both semi-naked (for pre-approval) and (every day which Percy has to see). On one trip, Lynne finally chose an elegant molded 32D cup size Avero style bra, in a checkerboard pattern, café latte color, and for panties, two virtually transparent matching small panties in thong and a very short tight hot pant style. For under evening gowns, she chose a nude color, polyester/spandex size 6 strapless full slip and for the swimwear, an Exotica model, single piece, leopard print all-in-one suit with plunging a V neck, size 6, with lots of breast cleavage and exposure.

To retell the hour-long program in the changing room, it went like this: The room had a daybed, pillows, bathroom with a shower. Lynne took everything off, including shoes; stood there naked in, what she called, *everyday sameness*, looking out the window. The sales lady had brought in multiple selections for Lynn to try on; first, from naked *sameness*, to second, naked *newness* and then to semi-naked *newness*...all for approval by me. In truth, I said, *'I like naked sameness/ naked newness better than either semi-naked version;* so Lynn skipped trying on all the rest of lingerie, purchased the total nakedness version, and we went home to her new after shopping program she promised.

When we reached her home, I carried all packages to the bedroom and went to the kitchen for iced tea. Later, Lynne appeared to share some iced tea wearing only a bra, panties, and a robe. She asked me to unhook her, took me by the hand and said, *"How about a real naked event I promised myself while my husband is away on a business trip; I'll instruct you."*

"Of course, I'm a fast learner. Wait, is that someone at the door?"

$\sim$

Total Surprise Massage

Explicit Commentary

After Rush Hogarth founded his first Spa, called *Knead-Me*, with his office on the second floor, he often looked out the window and watched the action on the tennis courts in the early morning always knowing it's going to be a glorious day when there are only a few clouds on the horizon, the temperature is just seventy and the regular morning wind off the ocean is not yet a factor. The feather palms beyond the courts, by the coast highway, are barely moving. Rush sees that neither the play in the senior men's doubles game on court number three to his left nor the singles match between the two very athletic women on court number one, immediately below his window, are not affected by any breeze. He knows the women will quit playing when the wind starts; wind contributes to a bad hair day.

As he continues to watch the women playing, they are not only aggressive but good looking, have great figures and he hopes when their last game is over, they will come in for a massage by using the newly opened full-service women's spa section of *Knead-Me*. He knows that attractive women, like those he is watching now, will attract more women to the spa.

"Is everything packed in the Lexus RX300?"

"Yes, PH, I got everything out, double checked it and Joe Bob put all the stuff in the Lexus for you. That includes your portable massage table, its head rest, a caddy of oils and supplies, a bag filled with some customer wraps, standard flannel table covers and massage table pillows."

Since founding *Knead-Me*, Rush rarely gives massages other than for a few special male clients...he doesn't have time, and he certainly is not keen about making any *house* calls either. But fair is fair, and Hal Thompson is one of my best customers, a generous tipper who brings in a lot of business that helps put the spa in the black and on the road to success. Still, a last-minute request yesterday afternoon to go to Hal's *home* early this morning is unusual because Hal's regular routine is either, I go to Hal's *office*, or he comes directly to the spa, or pad as Cynthia calls it. However, today is a projected slow morning so I agreed to drive up to Hal's, house, give him a thorough massage, and be back in plenty of time for this afternoon's appointment with the venture capital people from northern California, near Stanford University, who are interested in my *growing chain of spas* that need financial capital.

He calls to Cynthia, "Ok, I'm on my way."

"Right, see you later. Be sure to recheck the address, on the map I drew and the special parking instructions. The information I got over the phone when the appointment was made. Also note, the Thompson's house isn't easy to find, and they are very fussy about parking at their pad," Cynthia said.

Rush sat in the Lexus and reviewed Cynthia's notes: Hal's home is in Pelican Vista, part of the very exclusive, gated community section that overlooks the ocean and the Marina; also, there is a special request not to park in front of Hal's wrought iron entry gate to the home or in front of the driveway to the garage next to Hal's house and office which is part of the garage.

Rush stops at the security guard gate-office in Pelican Vista gives his name and destination to the guard and is approved to enter.

He drove beyond the house entry and the garage, and pulls up and parks. He unloads all his equipment, walks back to a call button recessed in the wall next to a speaker, pushes it and waits.

A voice said, "Yes? Please talk into the speaker."

"Hello, I'm Rush Hogarth to see Mr. Thompson. He's expecting me. I personally give Mr. Thompson massages and stress reduction rubdowns at his office or at my spa. Late yesterday an appointment was made for Hal to have a massage today here at his home."

A buzzer sounds the gate unlatches and swings open. Rush picks up the massage table, eases through the gate which shuts automatically, and locks behind him. He navigates a set of steps that lead to an interior flagstone patio and walks towards the front door. It opens, and a younger woman greets him.

"Hi, I'm Chloe Thompson," she said.

Rush is surprised. Chloe Thompson is much younger than Hal.

"Harry...oh, I guess you call him Hal...is away, some place in New Mexico. And obviously he didn't have time to call you and cancel his appointment."

"Chloe, who is it?" a voice from inside the house said. "It's a, Mr. Rush Hogarth, Hal's spa person who's come all the way out here with all his equipment to give Hal a massage; and Hal forgot to call and cancel."

"Well, why don't you at least ask him in for a cup of coffee and a croissant, Chloe, so his trip isn't totally for nothing?"

"Great idea, Jan, can you come in, Mr. Hogarth?"

"Yes, but please, call me Rush. I'll drop all my massage stuff out here."

"No, please leave all your things here in the entry hall," Chloe said stepping aside.

Chloe is gorgeous: medium height, sensuous figure, raven-colored hair, deep brown eyes, and sensational legs and bust. She is dressed in white: a deep, U-neck tank top with narrow straps, one of which she keeps adjusting, along with her matching material tennis shorts with high cut legs, plus tennis shoes and an obvious, semi-visible, special bra that obviously is not designed for serious tennis match play. It's her stretch material tank top and briefs, with a bare midriff in between, up to her chest level, which leaves little to the imagination. Chloe exudes sexuality; she is very aware of the effect she creates.

"Come on you two, I've set up everything here in the breakfast room," Jan calls to them.

Chloe leads the way. Rush follows admiring the scene; a view that certainly beats only girl-watching from his office window.

In the breakfast room, Chloe makes the introduction: "Rush, this is my neighbor from across the street, Janice Morgan, just call her Jan. We've been playing tennis on the court behind her house, just got back, and I've not had a chance to change. Also, it's the maid's day off so if you were ten minutes earlier, we wouldn't be here at all."

"Certainly, my lucky day, meeting both you lovely ladies and being invited in for some coffee and croissant, too," I said.

"Would you like an English muffin Rush, instead of a croissant?" Jan said.

"Only, if you're having some. Please don't go to any extra trouble for me."

"It's no problem. Oh, I guess I'll also have an English muffin instead of the croissant; how about you, Chloe?"

"Neither one for me, Jan," Chloe said.

"I suggest you all sit down while I toast the muffins?" Jan said while dropping two muffins in the toaster oven on the table and pouring three cups of coffee.

"How long have you been in the massage/spa business, Rush?" Chloe said.

"About six years now, Mrs. Thompson."

"Oh, please, call me Chloe."

"Ok."

"You have a chain of outlets started, don't you?" Jan said.

"Yes, I'm operating in all the sunshine states, and especially in places where there are up-scale resorts and sports activities."

"What sort of services do you offer? I don't know anything about what you do except for what Harry says, and he thinks you are a very smart entrepreneur," Chloe said.

"I'll try to be brief. First, we offer basic massage like you'd find at any well-run spa, second, we have physical fitness programs, and third, we perform sports injury and physical therapy, but only as prescribed by competent, licensed professional like me. We started as a provider of services just for men, but the last three years we've expanded our facilities and personnel to accommodate women. Quite frankly, women are better customers for basic massage and, of course, the services they receive at salons. We are just now getting into that phase of operations by modifying our physical facilities and seeking out the best personnel we can find, especially body hair specialists with an established following. Our expansion requires substantial capital."

"That's very impressive, Rush. How did you get into this type of business?" Jan said.

"And how did you pick, *Knead-Me*, as the name for your chain?" Chloe interjected, "I think it's very clever."

"I'll answer Janice's question first."

"Please, use, Jan."

"Ok, Jan it is. I was in college majoring in sports therapy and pre-med... and also taking some art classes...pottery and sculpture, that sort of thing. One of the coaches noticed I have exceptionally strong hands and fingers when I worked on any football players. I guess the strength came from the art classes. So, I got the idea of giving female/male massages to earn spending money. I bought some medical books on massage and success followed. I am making really good money, and that lead to the realization that I can make more money owning a massage facility/spa than just giving massages myself. The idea for a chain of spas happened later."

"As for the name, Chloe, I was writing a term paper for an English Lit class and it just popped into my mind. My timing was right as people had more money for recreation, sports, physical fitness and working out. Everything caught on. I believe the name really does bring the people in, but you also have to have the best personnel and service."

"Harry tells me you are his idea of what a son would be like if he ever had one—he admires your success. Are you married, Rush?"

"That's kind of you to tell me Hal's sentiments, Chloe, and no, I'm not married."

"How's the bottom, Chloe? You took quite a spill," Jan said.

"Only a bit sore but I'll get in the Jacuzzi and that should do it."

"Well, I have an idea. Why don't you have Rush give you a massage while he's here? He is a state licensed Physical Therapist, and I'll stick around to be the chaperone. There's no use his coming all the way out here with all that equipment without doing 'his thing' and after all, being paid. What do you guys think?"

"That's a great idea, Jan. Harry says Rush is exceptional, and I really prefer a masseur. Is that ok with you, Rush?"

"That would be fine because Jan is here," Rush said. But he does know it's not usual for a woman to be given a massage and choose a masseur, let alone in her home and not at a spa or beauty salon under controlled circumstances. He is really apprehensive about the idea, but figures he'll work fast, and everything will be all right with Jan there. Also, there is plenty of time…it's only about ten…and the meeting with the venture capitalists is not until two-thirty.

Chloe gets up from the kitchen table, shows Rush the bedroom that's on the same floor as the breakfast room; points where to set up the massage table: for privacy, away from a large sliding glass door that opens up on a patio overlooking the ocean and the marina, but where there is still plenty of light.

Rush gets his equipment, unfolds, sets up the portable table, and spreads the flannel cover over the padded surface. He hands Chloe a kimono, a body wrap and a special spandex, massage size panty. He is glad the panty is part of the usual supply in the bag Cynthia gives him. He feels less nervous.

Jan sits in a comfortable chair near the head of the massage table. Chloe said she'd change in the bathroom and disappears. She emerges in the kimono, the body wrap wound tightly around her, over the kimono and carrying a bath towel as she showered *before* the massage but *after* this morning's tennis work out.

"Please excuse the unmade bed and messy room, Rush, but I didn't expect to be getting a massage in my bedroom after tennis."

"No problem, Chloe. I'm even worse when it comes to housekeeping," Rush said smiling.

"I want a creative massage as I'm pretty stiff after all the tennis. Do you have some unscented oil with you?" Chloe said while she started to loosen off her wrap and kimono.

"Yes. Unscented is all I carry because men, like Hal, that I still do don't care for any perfume scent when they go back to business. I'm going to wash my hands while Jan gets you set on the table. I'll use the kitchen," Rush said.

Chloe drops the body wrap and kimono, puts her hands behind her head, stretches out, fully nude, and sits on the massage table, swinging her legs up and rolls onto her stomach...Jan picks up the wrap and covers Chloe completely as she is swinging her legs. Rush returns, adjusts the wrap making sure it drapes equally on both sides of the massage table and over Chloe's body. He asks her to move so her face fits snugly into the donut-style head rest which extends beyond one end of the table. This special design is an aid for breathing so the person getting the massage can lay flat, with arms along-side the body and the neck aligned; Rush folds down her wrap so only Chloe's neck and the tops of her arms and back are exposed; he ties his oil and supply caddy around his waist, takes a small bottle of unscented oil, opens it and applies some to Chloe's exposed skin. Her skin is in superior condition: smooth, soft, and obviously never subject to sunbathing like that of the beach-loving coeds Rush sees regularly. In fact, her skin, no argument about it, is the finest he's ever seen and touched.

"Chloe, you sing out if I massage too enthusiastically."

"Sure will, Rush. Also, if you're being too gentle," Chloe said moving her arms and raising herself up on her elbows to make sure she can be heard. While doing this, she briefly exposes her breasts. It's a spontaneous movement, but it creates a view of Chloe no one could miss.

Rush begins to massage with a kneading, pulling technique—working across Chloe's muscles and feeling to detect strength, tone or any soreness. He cautions himself, *be careful*, you're doing a woman not a male.

"Your hands and fingers are quite strong. Best I've ever experienced."

"That's from years of working with clay. I did that even before I went to college."

Within minutes, Rush is very surprised that he finds no evidence of any stiffness, soreness or unusual stress in any of Chloe's neck, shoulders or upper back muscles; it is as if she rarely engages in any serious exercise like tennis.

After another twenty minutes, he massages all of Chloe's arms, hands, fingers, neck, and back down to her waist. As he works, Rush eases off Chloe's body wrap as necessary, making, doubly certain her body covers are above the waist, her heavenly body waist, which is superb everywhere. Rush *bets she practices Yoga and stretching exercises. Despite her arms being mostly by her sides, except when he massages them and her hands and fingers, as he moves from one side of the table to the other, he sees the sides of each of Chloe's breasts as they are pressing against the table. No silicone there.*

"I'll finish now by doing all parts of your bottom, lower legs and all of each foot including the arches," Rush said moving the wrap completely from above the waist upward to the bottom of her neck, leaving Chloe only completely half-nude.

"Okay, so you guys are making progress, Chloe, but I'll stay until you take another shower then I'll have to go home and change to meet Mary Lou and Nora for lunch at Neiman's. I'll put your kimono and a dry bath towel at the foot of the massage table."

Chloe lifts herself up again, fully exposing her breasts as she talks to Jan, "Ok, Jan, stay till I'm set for my shower which is once I've got my kimono on to go to the shower, then you can sure leave and get ready for lunch."

With her breasts still exposed, it isn't till Chloe sees Jan sit down again that Chloe lays face down on the massage table again. Rush appreciates the bare breasts event; he thinks, *A perfect ending, I'll do her feet and lower legs quickly and be out of here…*he begins to move to the lower end of the massage table when Chloe said, "Don't forget to do my hips, feet again, and bottom Rush; I'm still tender because of the fall I took over at Jan's because feet take a real beating in a tennis match." At the same time, Chloe lifts her right leg, kicks at the body wrap now covering her and pushes it until it slides down toward the foot of the massage table: leaving her entire back, buttocks, thighs and legs…*everything*, fully bare and exposed.

Rush is startled…not only by Chloe's statement and sudden actions, but because he confirmed she is not wearing the massage-style panty he gave her. For seconds, Rush stands there admiring even more views of the rest of Chloe's…naked body.

"Come on, Rush, you've seen those college girls bare-assed and all over before. Get started," Chloe said

"Right," he stutters and begins applying oil on Chloe's hips, buttocks and legs, then using a closed fist, rolling, kneading technique, interspersing it with each hand formed like a cup, when, with fingers extended, he presses deeply, then grasps, and pulls her entire body: hips, top of the buttocks, cheeks, and always massaging across Chloe's butt muscles, at the same time.

Chloe spreads, adjusts her legs slightly and said, "Don't forget the tailbone. It's really tender because that's what hit the court first as I fell."

"Ok," Rush said, adding some oil to Chloe's skin, being careful not to let any of it run down and get between her legs. He turns his right hand on edge, presses down on top of the tailbone area and pushes Chloe's entire body, not just part of it, toward the top of the table. At the same time, he uses a pulling and grasping massage method again on each butt cheek, one cheek at a time. This works well since Rush is standing facing Chloe's right hip as it lays on the table, and he feels what he is doing is the least intrusive and best under the circumstances of her now fully directed massage.

Chloe raises herself slightly on her elbows to be sure Rush hears her and said, "Feels great, but you should also position one of your hands flat on my bottom, with pressure on the cheeks for control and massaging lightly again toward my waist." After giving these instructions, Chloe pushes herself down from the top of the massage table, away from the donut-face fixture, raises and crosses her arms above her shoulders and puts her forehead on her hands.

Rush, in following instructions places his right hand on her bottom. He's nervous and thinks of several things: *the protection of Jan is there but she does not see anything is wrong yet to mention it, and he is seeing and rubbing parts of Chloe Thompson he should not be viewing and massaging, and he needs to get out of there...fast.*

"Shift your hand down, along my bottom more toward my legs and rub a little lower. You're not getting the entire area."

He thinks, *why worry, if this is what Chloe Thompson wants, get with the program, but the massage is now one hundred percent run by Chloe and that might cause problems now and later.* And so, Rush begins to ease his right hand down alongside Chloe's right cheek, which adjusts her legs slightly, till his technique penetrates enough until he feels his hand slide and gently touching more new skin areas.

"That's it, just great. Keep it up," Chloe murmurs as she kicks off most of the rest of the body wrap so she is lying on the massage table completely naked. Rush continues massaging all sides of Chloe's bare open legs.

Chloe moans and said, "Roll me slightly toward you, Rush, so I'm lying on my right hip. That way you can continue to see all of me. It's also reacting to tennis so don't be afraid of countering and massaging all of me."

Chloe shudders and rolls left off her hip and onto her back; as quickly as she does this, Rush moves to her legs to massage them again.

"Do my abdomen area while I'm lying on my back; also, the sternum bone between the breasts."

"That does it," Rush said, "but first we need to put a small, flat table pillow under you to accent your bottom and hips."

So, promptly Chloe bends both legs, puts her feet on the massage table, next to her torso, pushes and raises her body off the table between her feet and shoulders so Rush slips the pillow under her. Rush admires her maneuver and his new view. He pours oil on Chloe's shoulders, breasts and entire abdomen as Chloe lays flat again. Rush begins to lightly move his hands over her body between her neck and the top of her frontal bikini area, using only a slight, grazing touch. Chloe flushes about the neck, face and breasts...everywhere. Rush spends more time massaging the front of Chloe's body which is now exposed. She cooperates by raising and crossing her arms above her head, alternating placing her hands underneath the key parts of her body so that she accentuates everything getting attention and by bending and pulling again her legs upward along each side of her body up to and opposite each breast; I think, *what a lucky guy Hal is, his lady is sexually active and has the body and athletic desire to go with it; as no doubt, few women have.*

Chloe interrupts Rush's reverie, saying "First, massage all of the entire length of my bare legs again like you were doing. Then, I'll need the Kimono to go then, as both of us are satisfied with everything so far, and any more massaging will only concentrate on areas of me that I don't want to include in my massage today. I think all we need do now is shower, remove any excess oil while we concentrate on special massage areas and to adjourn for lunch and let Jan go home to change for her lunch date.

"Rush you use the shower first; I'll be along after I stretch, relax, catch my breath; use the advice my GYN gave me and hum that song in the *Bond* movie that says it: *Nobody does it better, baby, you're the best*; Rush gets up, goes into a large magnificent marble shower, undresses, starts the shower, begins soaping, washing his hair and through the glass shower door he sees Chloe lying naked on the table doing stretching exercises, inserting something until between her legs until Jan covers her with a body wrap. He watches puzzled. Then Chloe naked, opened the shower door, gives Rush a smile and said, "While you are naked, Rush, wash me front and back with this unscented, bath gel; be careful, the breasts, are more sensitive after more than the regular amount of attention."

Rush follows instructions, gets out of the shower, dries, dresses and packs up all his equipment. Soon Chloe finally comes out of the bathroom, still naked and tells Rush, "Do blot any excess wet areas I missed, especially like under my breasts, arms and between my legs. Rush continues to follow instructions and addresses all areas mentioned.

Chloe gets a Lycra, smooth cup, nude color, Miracle bra and some panty hose from a bureau, and said, "Rush, be a dear and fasten the bra for me. I never get these things hooked up correctly. Oh, and before I forget, Jan, wants a massage just like mine since you do come out to the house. Do you have a private number she can use?"

"Yes, I have a direct number. It's on a card I'll leave with you."

Chloe puts the bra straps over her shoulders and turns around so that Rush can hook her up. He reads the label, *Neiman Marcus, 32-D, Special Order*. "How do you want it, Chloe, tightest, middle or first row?"

"Better make it tightest as I'm wearing the décolleté white sheath dress later which needs that full-bosom look," Chloe said.

After he hooks her up, Chloe leans forward and lifts and adjusts each breast to fit it into the cups. Next, she sits down in a chair and works her way into sheer-to-the-waist panty hose. After staging the lingerie performance, Rush is ready to go back to the massage table or whatever might be next; Chloe is very aware of what Rush is thinking. Next, she needs help with the white sheath dress; the dress with the full-bosom display that is just short of illegal because each of her nipples are both semi-visible. And finally, with Rush and Jan holding her hands, for balance as she explains it, Helen slips into her shoes.

"Look, Chloe, you can't carry things to the Lexus dressed as you are. I can handle everything. It's no problem."

"Did you park beyond the garage?"

"Yes."

"Well, I can let you out through the garage. That will make things simpler; just use cash for the massage."

"The cost will be my standard rate I would have charged, Hal. Cynthia, will call you."

Rush checked the time; he had plenty to be ready for the talk with the Capital experts, coming from Stanford, and to get to get Chloe to the meeting in her 32-D Bra and dress, sheath style, to be at that meeting with the Stanford personnel; and be able to influence the success, of Rush's part, with my female contribution for the spas in partial payment for the great massage he gave me while I did the great breast and nude displays I put on. I'm sure Jan wants a similar event.

Trophy Wife Trap

Explanation

Cynthia comes into Rush's office and said, "Hal Thompson is down in massage room F and wants to see you, RH, he really looks upset."

Rush goes into room F and finds Hal sitting on the massage table. "What's wrong, Hal? You look stressed out, worried."

"I have to give you some background, Rush. We've known each other quite a while, so I can trust you. Well, you've never been up to my home...so if you had, you would know I have two master bedrooms; one for Chloe... that's my wife, and one for me. When I get back, about a month ago from a quick trip to New Mexico where I made a fortune on some gas wells, but that's another story. And the night I come back Chloe slips into my bedroom wearing a see-through nightgown and crawls into bed with me. This is unusual, but what's more unusual, we have sex. It's the first time in quite a while. I didn't know I could really do the thing anymore, but if you saw Chloe in a see-through nightgown, you would know how you could perform. She can turn on a corpse. And wouldn't you know it, she's pregnant. And what's more it may be twins."

"So, what's bad about that, Hal? You've always talked about not having children; especially about not having a son."

"Yeah, yeah, Rush, but that means a long time ago, not at my age. And then there's a very ugly thing that happens around here."

"What's that, Hal?"

"It's called the Trophy Wife trap that my buddies warned me about. I just hope it's not what is happening to me."

"Explain your take on the Trophy Wife trap."

"That's where an older guy, like me, marries a young, very beautiful gal…that's what Chloe is, of course, you should see her. And before the marriage you have an understanding that both agree to, 'No Children,' but the Trophy Wife sets it up, gets pregnant…by me her husband."

"I still don't see the problem. What happens that's so wrong?"

"I'll tell you what's wrong. The Trophy Wife has a baby and then the older husband gets taken to the cleaners in a divorce and is left alone. It's like a disease. Listen to this: Chloe's best friend is a gal named Jan Morgan. She lives across the street from us, so Chloe and Jan are thick as the proverbial thieves. Well, Jan is also pregnant. It's like an epidemic up there. And Jan files for divorce already, and the baby is not due for something like seven more months. Imagine it, seven months till birth and now a divorce. You think you're a smart, smooth, savvy businessman, but the Trophy Wife takes you to the cleaners, never even looks back. But maybe, just maybe you love your wife, it's not the money…*you can always replace money*, but you lose the wife and the baby, too, you can't replace that."

"I'm sure everything will work out fine, Hal. I'll give you an extra, special massage today to work out stress and relax you. How's Mrs. Thompson handling being pregnant, by you?"

"Just great, happy, very happy; and maybe that's what worries me, too. I don't know?"

⌐·╫╫╫╫·⌐

Rearrange Lynne,
Sex Position Shopping

"Do we have time for another session, Percy?"

"Sure, but you rest an hour, Lynne, before we start again."

"Great idea; however first, turn me over on my stomach so I can use my knees and elbows and raise my bottom and upper body structure, so you can reach under me and alternate breast, bottom massaging and maneuvering me, until I'm totally in the desired position for you to give me perfect attention. Also, be sure to control your actions so you can tell me if you're seeing and enjoying everything, both visible and partly hidden, by my design in our new exercise program.

"Ok, let's shower, now and then I have question for you."

Lynne at Neiman Marcus

"Saw you at *Neiman Marcus* yesterday with, Lynne, Percy. Did she buy a lot of clothes; she has very expensive taste; did you drive her home, too?" Victoria said.

"Yes, Victoria, Lynne had quite a lot of packages and did not want to wait for store delivery since she wanted *some* of what she bought to wear right away."

"Maybe you can take me next week, say *Wednesday* next; I feel a *Sameness/Newness Cycle* coming up. Does Lynne get your opinion about what she buys?"

"*Some*, but it's mostly the color of a dress or how she might look in it when she carries it on a hanger to try it on in a changing room; she holds up in front of her before she goes in to try it on; I'm certainly not much informed about lady's clothes so basically I drive her over and back and help with packages."

"Ok, if you can take me to *Neiman Marcus*, I'll need about two hours for shopping and extra time for the commute and for us to go to lunch… the store opens at 9AM."

"Victoria, we are set, except I can't do lunch as I have another customer at noon."

"Alright, so, here's the plan, I'll be sure to finish shopping in two hours sharp…9AM to 11AM then you take me home. I'll buy you lunch on another day."

"Ok, we're all set, let's go."

Timing Victoria

Percy knew Victoria was his first customer today, but he figured he can get her on time as always. The center of attraction, prompt Lynne, would be ready at noon sharp to begin her shopping spree; he's correct and everything looks to be on schedule for getting Lynne per schedule until Victoria hits the lingerie selection and stops to pick out a new bra/panty set…"Something to wear under a cocktail dress," she said. "Then, finally," she adds, "I need a new swimsuit, which is the next selection area. I won't need to try it on though, as I know what fits me. I will try on the new bra/panty set to see if I like it, as it's a make I've never bought before."

"Don't get a chill in the changing room. I'm sure everything will look great."

"Not to worry, Percy, I'm fine and we will still be on time for the rest of our schedule and yours."

Juggling the Women

Percy thought, while taking Victoria all the way to her home, that his juggling plans with her (and Lynne later today) put him in a risky situation, and he sure didn't want to lose Lynne since he had no *naked sameness*, or just plain *all nakedness* experiences, like at Neiman Marcus, or *complete nakedness* with Victoria at any time, or anywhere else, as I do with Lynne; so, this *Sameness/Newness Cycle*, or 'good for us' feeling, as in The Garden of Eden, could unravel everything unless sometime later, if I don't get Victoria home and am not on time to get Lynne; and I can't persuade Victoria to agrees to some sort of Commitment, or 'good for us' understanding. The facts are: Lynne likes nakedness, period, lots of it, and plenty of sex, as if that's her exclusive Control and Obsession technique; what if she is seeing at least one other guy, and if she has any hint, I've got another shopping partner, when she assumes she is in complete control…then I'm also through. I'm also done, if to her, Lynne thinks commitment means, at any time, she has a right to say goodbye. Ok, maybe Lynne believes she does have control and can walk away unhurt, but a loss always means hurt; and any act of choosing is never easy and absent consequences, so always prompt

Lynne' is the better assistant; but, can we build a life built only on sex and have it be 'good for us', permanently?

Center of Attention

But, sex propelled Lynne into believing she was the center of attention, not to worry, and avoid believing she is a *victim*. So how, did she achieve being the center of attention? She wore clothing that drew attention to her body, especially ample breasts, *with provocative emphasis, which was realistically saying, I'm available.* Also, behind her message was a personality trait, an obsession she has that *"has to rely on sex to control and survive in this world, of self-character attention, as if it is we who really do have a world of self-alienation.* As one famous psychologist describes it under the topic: CONCEPT OF NARCISSISM, thank you, doctor.

Eager Aggressive

She deals in densities of guile
As Goebbles did in lugen…Lies.
And her bold, brazen attacks,
Are blunt sexual acts
Of manipulation.
"Coitus, she says, is the situs
Of suasion, make each event
Succinct, sure
And all will inure
To your legends
Of temptation."

"So, why envy,
Lust after
Her game?
Dauntlessness is nature's
Choice of roles
Which holds:
A female
Of a kind,
Always glows
When semen
Overflows."

Dangerous Time Fragments II

With opportune direction
Love, enchanted sat with us
Pausing amid her fragile
Choices of variable feelings:
Passion, Acceptance,
Disenchantment,

And Guile...
But God, giving us free will
Watched us,
Waited, and waited,
And retired.

Fragment: Experience

Commentary

With the aid of all his resources, knowledge and judgment in Title Industry pricing industry experience and files of documentation, Keith figured our journey begins as a series of *Fragments*; (some planned/ some unplanned) with some more vivid than others, which means we recall them more easily because they seem to last longer in our memory while others, that we might recall, have faded into short term recall and we *choose* not to remember them.

We often divide *Fragments* into periods like, schools: Elementary, High, College, Graduate; or Military, and so forth; as we also use marriages, divorces, successes, failures, disappointments and whatever strikes as appropriate as life moves on.

We also split Fragments into friendships; lives of our children before or after leaving home; family activities; the frequency and speed of the passage of life; and how certain fragments come and go or fade into memory; or just plain disappear. We also like to go into what we call *continuous* Fragments: such as taxation, home repairs, trips to the grocery store, banks, or always infrequent trips, unpleasant events, like the dentist. There are Fragments, too, which have special expressions: *Death is easy, living is hard, and the car insurance went up again...how much?*

Fragment: Reality, 1982-1983

Commentary

Our Present reality may dictate many *Fragments*: However, sometimes, if ever, *Fragments* are connected or are just random by happenstance or cause, especially, by factors not under our control.

Current events also dictate many fragments. For example: The Middle East Mess, cost of the Welfare State, *Sameness/Newness*, the content of short stories and novellas in many published books and over 100 published poems contained therein; and, of course, how life and culture profoundly influence our journey with all the episodes and fragments it generates that become part of our life's voyage and its fabric. *So, give us a definition of just one Fragment that was not caused by you, but you had to cope with: Moving, by 1939 to and from: Michigan, Pennsylvania, California and Colorado, which meant living in more than a dozen locations and homes while attending an equal number of new schools.*

'Ok, what were the disappointments'? *Loss of friends and teachers I got to know, constant changes in curriculum content, and the fact that at one school I was classified as a potential problem student because of so many school changes, disliked by students who thought they ran the place, because I was new and interrupted the existing pecking order; and finally I had no place to call home; also the constant travel during WWII which was different and difficult because of troop transport, especially into and out of Chicago…loss of valued time with my sister, when we were separated, because she was older and always loved and helped me. We were never able to restore this closeness again, after being separated in High School.*

Fragment: Adulthood

Commentary

Then complex adulthood begins with formidable fragments which are often frequently generated by others who create problems such as sophisticated gender sensitive stubborn matters that are usually absent solutions. In recent years communication could generate peace; however, when a happenstance event occurs, and negatives become common, so encountering that event may produce bad results, counter to lasting relationships; for example, a warning that an environment is negative, if ignored and not understood, said event, *named possible trouble,* can occur and cause a change in life plans, making a new fragment named *Disaster*. As Ray Bradbury warns us in his lectures: *people who put you down or insist you change are not your friends: separate yourself from them before positive fragments are gone forever.*

Recall how in the movie Pretty Woman, there is a discussion of this between Vivian and Edward. While they are lying next to each other, naked, in bed, she is telling Edward how she was the victim of negative input and how she dealt with it. Who wouldn't listen under such ideal circumstances? Especially as the scenes continue and Vivian is the victim of unkindness while trying to get a dress to go out to dinner. Edward rushes to her defense by telling her people are nice to Credit Cards, not people; so, he takes her shopping, credit card in hand, helps her, and proves his point.

Fragment: Paradigm Shift

In 1965, a paradigm cultural shift continued in the US when the Greed-raider style in executive management style began and continued. It was a significant process that pushed Raiders to *get* money rather than by the traditional style of executives *earning* money the old-fashioned way through key planning, budgeting, rewarding productivity gains, training employees and keeping them, etc. A popular example: the movie, *Pretty Woman,* released in 1990, is a classic, step by step lesson in a Raider creating a leverage buy out, starting the sale of target parts and land to pay for more of the buy-out process, followed by the sale of the entire target to *get* money by proving the target is worth more sold in pieces than as a whole. A real life early parallel of this strategy is the recent raid and destruction of *Title Insurance & Trust Company, which had its headquarters in Los Angeles and where the new CEO hired in 1982 was a Loot and Leave style expert until losses at a new subsidiary and a collapse in the value of mortgages insured forced a drastic modification of the Liquidate and Leave strategy.*

It's a noticeable phenomenon today that management styles of many executives are duplicates of the solutions they used in their environmental challenges and the upsets they faced as youngsters and in prior Raider failures. The constant movement of executives now from one disaster to another reflects their desire to achieve, prosper and receive praise in the press. But, it also tells us individuals are searching to find operating patterns which 'mirror' the successful methods used by some new executives to respond to older situations by adopting, where possible, the means which will significantly alter the environment in a company, as it did alter it, when the Raiders were growing up and achieved some success.

This will not necessarily result in the best solutions for all other personnel in today's world and, in fact, may cause substantial turnover in employment, frustration, apprehension, fear and a systemic weakening of the business and loss of the best employees who seek safety. In extreme cases, the atmosphere the executive creates will be the very one he engineered at his last position that he wanted to avoid again by changing companies; when this occurs, the Raider is caught in a vicious cycle which he is at a loss to explain when he faces: turnover, declining productivity, profits, and apprehension, fear, failure in communications, and a predictable end of his new employment.

In this sort of a situation there is always a search for a scapegoat and, most often, the real cause, is the CEO himself, who is ignored as the top guy has a severance contract and his own Board of Directors who do not want to be forced to pay his contract cost and admit the mistake they made in hiring him in the first place.

Our scapegoat thinks, *they were all for my aggressive style, attention to micromanaging reputation and my own internal analysis shows: I considered, how did my plan go wrong? I gave them just what they wanted: A leverage buy out, sell off parts of the company and the land then sell off the best part of the company which is worth more as a stand-alone unit then with the balance still part of the whole. I used only the successful speeches rules from my early stuff, jobs: service, service, I'm in the Service Business, paper delivered on time, especially the Sunday one with the Sports Section, magazine for the lady of the house...no torn cover, carry change so I get paid on time, get tips, get money. I really followed that idea completely, especially the final sale to the people with cash. Also, the constant attack on the small internal Print shop where the Vice President there thwarted me every time along with all his computer systems, he somehow had installed that keeps all the operating unit Officers happy and exposes, traps a lot of the petty theft experts. Even the billing system he helped design with the aid of Accounting and the Class Action Law Suit he detected in time to stop it but I stepped in after huge losses, and was able to blame some others...not me; the out-side lawyers know of this and my informant warning me if we went to court, I'm finished; this guy's expert testimony would finish me.*

Cheated II

\Necessity tricked me,
Don't you see?
With all its sexual mysteries
That made my choice no choice
Since I pledged, too soon,
Life's afternoon
And became entrapped
In obligation's vise
Where I traded freedom
To flow, to play
In the field
Of the young,
Where time hung
Slowly in the sun;

Did the departure
Dispel your fury?
"Not to compromise,
Not to adjust...
All that money,"
She muttered.
"But night now ensues
And my anger waxes
At that obligatory vise,
Oh, I was controlled,
Then rejected,
Don't you see?
I'll not be manipulated twice."

Fragment: The New Structure of Title Insurance and Trust Company

On September 30, 1983, Title Insurance and Trust Company announced, at its corporate headquarters in Los Angeles, California, it was part of a new Leverage Buyout project of $271 million that would separate it from its current owner, Southern Pacific, and become two new Corporations: one to continue its leadership position in title insurance with a unit to be called Ticor, and a second new unit to be called TMIC, (Ticor Mortgage Insurance Company); both will be led by a new CEO named Winston, 'Bud' M.

The LBO will be undertaken in a series of steps that include a cash payment to Southern Pacific of $240 Million; a 13 ½ % subordinated promissory note; and 50 million of 14% of stock to Associated Madison; $190 million of Bank Loans; 110-115 by sale of current TI assets: the Print Network, real estate, the local Print Shop, TI's headquarters building at 6300 Wilshire and other real estate now considered surplus, like the new title headquarters building in Rosemead; a continuation of TI's 50 million of 9 ½ % debentures, due to remain outstanding until maturity in 2008. Sale of the Trust Depart is scheduled to occur later. Cost of debt on an annual basis is calculated to be $22,025,500.

Element, LBO Financial Figures

The LBO will consist of an investment group including executives from American Can, East Coast Investors and specialists in Mortgage Insurance from Fannie Mae and Freddie Mac, in Washington DC.

Element 2, Administration

The structure for the continuation of the title insurance company, Ticor, will be wither staffed by the potential buyer or by the transfer of all personnel, its Vice President and all the departments from the existing Administration Division located in Rosemead. This function, as mentioned, will report to Bud M. immediately or as provided later based on policy decisions after the sale of the rest of Title Insurance and Trust Company in March 1991. At the request of Chicago Title, the new owner of TICOR, the Vice President of Administration, will remain available until July 1, 1991, when he will retire on his anniversary after 30 years of employment with Title Insurance and Trust Company.

Fragment: Inner Conflicts

Prologue

There are executives today who seek only employees who are winners and are determined to eliminate all losers because the total of an entity is the sum of its parts. So, in new businesses, key officers review their work force to achieve maximum results by weeding losers from winners. These officers usually disagree on conclusions among themselves, but it is always select employees who receive either thumbs up or thumbs down ratings.

These practices depends greatly on bias, prejudice, or just plain like or dislike, but therefore, to analyze the present work, effort, output or achievement of others is one thing, but to develop a new rationale, philosophy or method, and then judge *its* output is indeed quite another task. The world is filled with analyzers who would have us believe that it is only their analysis and rearrangement of the effort of others that has real value.

Of equal interest, however, is the analyzer's belief, sustained by his mission and undetected rationalizations, that it is only *his function which orders and ordains the personal destiny of fellow men and events* so that just he can predict and verify a winner or non-winner...a loser: example, the unexpected failure by a consistent winner, often a person who has achieved, at say, the age of fifty...like in golf or business.

'A belief in a basic conflict within the human personality is ancient and plays a prominent role in various religions and philosophies.' *OUR INNER CONFLICTS*, Karen Horney, M.D., W.W. Norton & Company, Inc. 1945, p. 37ff

The Cast

Bud M., CEO, Nitpicking Limited, LLP
Paul Hartmann, Consulting Psychologist
Innocent Employees, Any Company

Part 1

After several interviews with Bud M., Paul Hartman realized he had not been hired to identify winners or losers, but to locate employees, at any level of responsibility, that Bud could not dominate or who impacted profitability; but it's individuals that Bud simply dislikes because they are simple threats to any one of his conscious conflicts: attitude, control, values or prejudices.

Paul saw Bud's conflicts as inconsistent behavior, like trying to get rid of valuable people who contribute to corporate success, just because they are at an age, he had a profound dislike for, (age 50+). Paul thought, *Bud's dislike is a hostile reaction, and he wants to absent himself from these employees by eliminating them. Of course, his action would appear to increase profitability as would firing any lower level cost personnel.*

The debates Paul had with Bud over certain firings made Paul consider he was not being professional, just wearing a mask, because to do otherwise might threaten the job he needed badly by making Bud uneasy and also because now it's Paul not accepting Bud's dominating propensity; and this would also focus on Paul's' not accepting Bud's conscious conflict resolution about control. Sure, Paul thought, *I'm following most of the goals Bud laid out for me, but I don't believe in him as a source of wisdom, and know I don't dare cross an authoritarian boss like Bud M.*

Further talks with Bud, however, began to show me how separated he had become from anyone around him, and that included me; I knew if I became a threat to his unconscious habit to be alone, just by himself, my assignment here as a consulting Psychologist was over. Bud was not only rejecting my suggestions, but he was no longer even polite about it. Obviously, my ideas did not coincide with his set of values.

I asked myself, *why was I being so stupid…just dumb up, ease by, become a better actor; what was I thinking? The answer was really clear: only be anxious to please, fill out my time and be on my way. I realized what is discouraging, often, about the business environment is the price a typical, or even special employee pays in living through the process some executives go through: it's really a constant demand that any employee must endure being a goat while the executive experiments in learning to manage; put one man in absolute power to run an hundred or more people, and he can wreck unexpected damage without the slightest awareness of what he is doing.*

I considered, *could it be that I looked at things more in an individual sense and less as people are just employees who are only worth so much in exchange, as Bud does, like assets and resources are, to be used in specific functions and if things change you do something about the assets or resources you are using? It wasn't normal for me to see individuals as mere exchangeable entities. To me, people are quite real as individuals, not just useful production units that are rotated just because of age.*

I was aware that Bud constantly was withdrawing from people and that some-how I had become a buffer that he tolerated even though he had a crucial need for closeness, which it would appear, he denied; my phone rang, it was Sara, Bud's secretary, he wants to see you tomorrow at 2:30 in his office…don't be late he hates to be kept waiting."

Part 2

"Come in, Paul, I'm glad you are available so I can review all you have accomplished. Please sit down."

"Thank you, Bud."

"As you are aware, I'm usually in private meetings which isolate me a great deal of the time from day-to-day management activities which gives me the freedom I need to look for opportunities to increase my profitability. First, I want to thank you for all the personnel replacements in Senior Staff that you accomplished, under my direction, of course, and I want you to know you have received full credit for all terminations, the last one to occur is later this afternoon; and all terminations are complete. Change is not my preference, so your help was essential and removes the need for future long-term actions to be directed by me."

"Thanks again, Bud."

"Second, it's no secret, I plan to marry, no dates set yet, but I'll include you in the list of attendees when plans are firm."

"Congratulations, Bud. Your marriage is good news."

"Third, I've been thinking of another assignment I know you will enjoy as you will have more independence doing it once I've set out all the parameters and reviewed in detail my directions for my goals in the project. I'll go over all this when my mind is made up and Sarah has everything typed up for me to review, step by step, as I present it to you later; I'll be in touch. Do you have any questions?"

"Just that I am please my efforts, so far, met your approval, and you have a project in mind for future profit."

"Good, Paul, let me conclude by adding that I believed you worked well with simplicity in your over-all performance, kept me aggressively in charge and you did not annoy me with any unwanted advice. I'll be in touch when I need to meet with you again as I must leave now with the last senior level termination schedule for today, Friday. In the meantime, you should take a well-earned week off starting next Monday and enjoy a vacation."

"Thanks again for the compliment and the approval of a one-week vacation."

I went back to my office well prepared with *the news* behind Bud's comments at the meeting: (1) he has no marriage in his immediate plans, (2) he is leaving right now so that it fits the charade that I am responsible for the senior staff terminations, (3) the *start* of my weeks' vacation is the *end* of my employment here, (4) Sara will have my final paycheck ready when I return a *week* from Monday, (5) no doubt Bud will have a new *consultant* on board, right here in this small office, come *next Monday*, when *my vacation starts* and employment end simultaneously, (6) Super Aggressive Bud is still totally in charge and ready to stretch his definitions of Honesty and Fairness to the limit, (7) Bud will continue to reduce labor costs with additional firings to satisfy his greed for a *well-earned salary* increase, and finally, (8) I will complete packing my personal property, private notes and be out of here as soon as Bud's departure is verified. I feel sorry for the half dozen low-paid employees in the small Print Shop who are, obviously, the next target for payroll reduction to be accomplished by the new *consultant*.

I put my two small boxes on the floor in the little closet where I hang my coat and walked over to the Contract Personnel office knowing bud would soon arrive to see I didn't leave early but would be there for the firing of the final older staff employee to be eliminated; firing was important because that meant retirement pension would be reduced.

As expected, Bud arrived. I turned my head away, so he was not aware that I had seen him in the small mirror on the wall. He looked everything over and left. After a proper time, elapsed, I went back to my desk and found a small note; 'Have a great vacation.'

Glancing at my watch, I saw it was 4:45. I retrieved my boxes and headed for my dinner appointment with Harry, at our favorite place, to exchange information and status. He was inside, seated at our usual two-party booth and having a drink. He saw me and waved. I sat down beside him.

"What's really happening, Paul, you look worse for wear?"

"I'm not sure that I can be certain about all of it, Harry, but somewhere between Bud's *conscious and unconscious motivations it struck me that the promise of what Bud could have been is gone.* I no longer feel any promise for him is going to be achieved. As for me, I've become an economic unit: simply, according to Bud, I am responsible for one function, firing employees that Bud picks out for termination, and I became the cover for Bud that makes it appear that I'm responsible for the whole show to reduce labor costs and boost profits in a dying company."

"Dying…?"

"Yes, that's the correct work…envy and greed has taken over."

"Then you're better off out of there."

"Absolutely, Harry."

"So, what's your next move, Paul?"

"Just what we've talked about the last couple of months, I open my consulting business on Monday taking advantage of the weeks' vacation that Bud just said I have coming…which I know is not true…I've just been fired and today was my last day."

"You're sure?"

"Yes, his secretary tipped me off and showed me my final paycheck… effective today, Friday, *before my unpaid vacation.*"

"Well. Good luck, Paul."

"Thanks, Harry. I'm going to be counseling all employees Bud has fired and using the money he will have to pay them since he is liable for using their age as the purpose for termination, which is not legal under current laws."

"How do you know all this, Paul?"

"Because I'm the one who had to prepare all Bud's termination papers that he had to sign."

―⁂―

Inner Conflicts

A subtle twist,
An off balancing thrust,
An absence of concern
For the terminated dust
That dirties the shoes
Of a CEO in a hurry.

Take care, soulless specialist
Of your corporate strategy:
You don't breathe, eat,
Sleep, procreate or tame
One unconscious moment
That your conscious ego,

Doesn't know:
That another specialist,
Isn't plotting and lying
For your demise, too.

Fragment: Chicanery, a Story - 1982

Commentary

With the aid of all his experience: title industry pricing, industry knowledge, and extensive documentation, Keith figures after Bud took over as the new CEO; Johnny resigns, following the rest of ownership senior officers. As Bud continues privatization of the ownership of the new Ticor (no outside stockholders), the road is now wide open to continue his "Loot and Leave" process for Ticor. By mid-1982, it's well underway and the overcapacity title insurance industry that was so vulnerable with its extra land holdings, expanded acquisitions, along with excess personnel to be fired or slowly weeded out.

Bud and his current actions are targeting: The Trust Company, the old Headquarters building on Spring Street, the big new facility at Rosemead, the Life Insurance unit, Jeffries Banknote Company, the administrative Services unit and its four independent functions, especially that pain in the neck…its Print Shop, along with the office supplies and warehouse, all at Rosemead. Scheduled to be subcontracted, with very favorable outside contract suppliers: Fleet, Purchasing, Forms Control, the System Six unit that does desktop publishing, and all in-house printing of Ticor operating procedures a certain officer letters…including my economy drive of elimination of the purchase of watches for 20 years of service, office parties at holidays as well as purchase of bottled water by the Print Shop which is required for mixing with ink to the presses.

But Bud knows he is getting impatient because of the time it was taking to achieve his entire program. He also believes it is better to use minor piece action than all at once actions; But Bud thinks I am, in fact attempting my program, to "Loot and Leave" Ticor as fast as I can. So, I needed to finally recognize, as well, that pricing in the title industry is complex, and requires attention to sophisticated land laws that are often impacted by politicians with devastating consequences in what has become a legal hobby: The Class Action Lawsuit. I was warned I needed to pay attention to my own Pricing Specialist who I ignored; this expert wrote letters, no one, especially me, paid any attention to him. Outside legal Counsel representing the people suing us, said, "Your, Administrative Services Vice President, was correct by millions of dollars." He was painfully correct!

Fragment: Human Nature, Risk Factors

Introduction

Underwriting parameters set by management in 1946-1991, in any given situation can determine who will be at risk as the amount level of insurance coverage that is under contract will indicate who it is: an individual or corporation. Example: the insurance purchased may only cover, a car, for example, only the *Manufacturer's* suggested cost; the Car *Dealer's profit is not included.* Therefore, usually an individual is at risk, for part of the *entire* cost of replacing the vehicle that is beyond repair. This is because the individual chose to buy only less expensive premium insurance; the insurance company did not receive sufficient money to set up a reserve, as required by the State Insurance Commissioner, to pay the cost of an entire new vehicle. In the case of a company, they may decide to carry less insurance to conserve cash and accept taking the risk. This same illustration applies to other forms of insurance such as flood, home owners, mortgage, personal property, umbrella casualty, within, of course, rules set by specific insurers where risk option is not available…as with current health insurance where risk rules are set as by the Federal Government.

Liquidate and Leave
Commentary

Keith is certain there is a pronounced feeling of Anger and a conscious malicious desire to harm others at Ticor who Bud believes thwarted his final attempt to get every penny out of a dying Ticor that he deserves for his brilliant plan to leverage buy it, sell it off in pieces, at a stunning profit, especially for American Can, and walk away, really rich, into the sunset. Of course, the stealing, loss of gross industry revenue and increases in losses hurt, but what really makes Bud furious is failure to sell off all the viable units in Administrative Services: land, equipment, excess staff and functions not wanted by the new buyer or to cut pension accruals: including that damn, well run Print Shop and the new computer unit, Systems 6, that does real desk top publishing and all new corporate procedures and operations publishing; Forms Control with a heavy input from Legal, Underwriting and all State Title Associations, Fleet Administration with all its the profit on the sale of over 1200 vehicles...especially the executive ones Bud had awarded with full knowledge of their future resale value; in addition, the usual surplus land sale at the soon to be sold building at Rosemead, including The Warehouse area, for storage of operating supplies, to be purchased by outsourcing, including land and shelving at Rosemead, for stored title files; also, if necessary, the extra land and shelving for the kitchen and cafeteria, at Rosemead etc. ; Bud knows how to get the best value he needs to recover at the final sale of Ticor to another title company, but to one that needs as much of the facilities that Ticor has that have been thinned down for a smaller size title company but still one with enough cash to buy out stock of Bud and his stockholder friends from the soon to be the Ticor stripped down to size, at both a reduced Rosemead and the corporate site on Wilshire.

Envy and Addiction
Commentary

Keith senses that the feeling of Anger at Ticor is really an addiction that has turned to hate; hate of management's program, really Bud's; secret goal, his *obsession*, to "Liquidate and Leave" Ticor as a shell of what it used to be. Bud's desire is lust-like to the extent of crude pleasure and sensual satisfaction to win at, no matter what the cost, to others or, no matter any advantage, 'Liquidate and Leave' might give to me and the small group around me, as illustrated by my constant, endless war and effort to get rid of the highly respected, well run, Print Shop, and the personnel who work there, which is really only a disguised lead into my getting rid of the of the entire Administrative Services Division and increase profits to me when all of the Title company is sold, according to my sale plans to outsource, at very favorable contract rates, all unneeded facilities, equipment and personnel at my terminal, final sale of what is left of Title Insurance and Trust Company.

Lust and Theft
Commentary

In truth, Keith, believes Bud has passed beyond any compulsion to appear perfect in his goals; he plain has to persevere to put the word *lien* on any assertions that he has failed, as in the past, so, once again he is following his 'Liquidate and Leave' strategy. Keith thinks Bud has to inflict emotional harm, too, like he did many times, even from childhood, but now his super ego demands he repeat. But to successfully feed it with a *triumph*; in fact, he has to have a *vindictive triumph* over others and remove any fear of his being unmasked and subject to contempt, ridicule, humiliation or anxiety. This need must repress everything that does not fit into his masquerade of achieving *all* his actual goals: especially 'Liquidate and Leave', while maintaining a façade of no cruelty or immoral behavior that Bud believes he does not practice at all and he is sure his personality will eventually protect him because he has no real, endless guilty feelings at all; since he is unaware of knowing what is happening and believes the comfort of his greed will protect him from false lies of hostility, cruelness and destructive envy from any of his radical changes to Ticor and hide him from him any inner conflicts that he is *totally unaware* he has anyway. I think Bud is hypnotized by his lust for success, while unaware of the neurosis which, I believe, is forcing him, against himself, to the point of creating frantic frustrations, within himself by always blocking, ever since childhood, time after time, any recognition that long ago he should have recognized by enjoying his own *Satisfaction* of conquering his own cycle of *Sameness* to *Newness*.

Growth

So, Bud recalled the talk he gave at the pep up meeting in Scottsdale, Arizona, where he gave a new plan outline; "We are going to grow the company," prior to those words, growth was not his goal; it was 'Liquidate and Leave.' Now it's 'Get the Assets', put them on the balance sheet, plus raises for everyone, including me; more executive level cars from Fleet Administration, that's another department the Print Shop VP also runs, and definitely the emphasis is on traditional 'let's make growth happen'; never mention 'Loot and Leave' or 'Liquidate and Leave' my real hidden goal.

Tully, Bud

Commentary

After an in depth briefing from my Senior VP advisor Tully, I relearn and recall that the Vice President of Administrative Services is not only just the executive in charge of the Internal Print shop but the annual, complex Fleet Administration program, models and pricing, and virtually all similar purchasing functions in the Title Insurance Company; also he does risk level high liability title order pricing with top senior title officers; the issuing of all company forms and procedures in coordination with legal and his specialists and other personnel connected with the internal running of our main business. The opinion of our legal staff, in working with out-side-council, is our Vice President of Administrative Services is rated a most out-standing officer. He is a Special Agent in the Inspector General Division of the USAF-OSI, on leave; a personal friend of the Secret Service Agent veteran I just hired to run our new security function; and our VP, Admin. Services also is on leave as a Senior Credit investigator for Chase Bank in NY; He is also the author of the documents that are the basis of the Class Action Law Suit which is being prosecuted against Ticor in the Trustee Sale Guarantee cases by Millar, Starr & Regalia that I dismissed when first brought to my attention; so far our losses are in the millions and I was urged by said Vice President, Ticor needed to amend the pricing of these Guarantees which I did not want to give up the revenue being generated from...they fit my plan's: objective...Liquidate and Leave, Ticor trimmed down and ready to be sold. I'll have more to say later after another briefing by my Senior VP Tully.

Fragment: Phoenix - 1953

Commentary

InMarch '53, prior to the Korean cease fire we knew was coming, Pauline and her sister Mary decided to link up by persuading Mary's husband, Jay, that when I'm out of the Service, we should move to Phoenix and live close to Pauline and Jay instead of my going back to New York and take the job that is waiting for me, per law, that make it easier for vets to be reemployed. The key to their plan is Mary's husband, Jay, a very successful Arizona businessman, is looking to start a new business venture in Phoenix and wants to find a *prospect with money* to join him. Jay is anxious to talk to me; and explain what he has in mind; he is going to be in New York City soon and hopes to schedule talks with me.

Jay sends me a hand-written letter in March with a proposition to meet with him at either The Union Club or The Metropolitan Club in April when I am on leave, depending on which club he decides to stay at. Jay follows up with an extensive typed letter documenting the gist of the content of what he has to say when we meet. It includes a plan for a business venture in Phoenix; the letter explains he is getting into a new business by buying a small Insurance company and a Real Estate firm that he wants me to operate and make profitable…he expresses his confidence that I will be successful.

In July, cease fire was agreements are signed to be effective at different times and dates in areas in Korea, like the fluid 8th Army front and the Permanent Panmunjom area, where extensive meetings have been held for a long time to stop the shooting. Immediately, I get another long, typed letter and documents from Jay saying that the financial picture is changing quickly in Phoenix with the cease fire...as if the war's over, so the prices he planned to pay for the insurance company and Real Estate outlet have doubled or tripled and he has already cancelled plans until things settle down.

For me and all of us in the OSI, we have already been alerted we will revert to reserve Status in the Air Force in July; unfortunately, I contacted my former employer that I will not be returning to my former job. I did this before talking to a couple of my former employee friends who told me the business climate in Phoenix dropped from great to disaster and to be sure to get back to my old job in New York because the word is out that any new ventures in Phoenix should only be done on 'a well-defined basis;' that's bank talk for 'look out.'

Jay's latest letter, also advised me to hang on to my former job because his plans are now on hold: for example, the surplus housing he was going to buy at Luke AFB is now gone; also because his bid was too late to be considered, so, as he said at our meeting, prices have already skyrocketed and quick profitability in Phoenix is over, and if I am nervous about a startup venture, I should stick with my current job; alas, the women's idea of living socially close together is over, too, and so is my former NY bank job. No mention, of course, about the money promised me.

Therefore, with temporary disappointment and flat broke we leave for California; I'm 26 and start three jobs that turn out to be: *Bank of America*, 1 year, *North American*, 6 years, and *Voit Rubber Company*, 3 years. Fortunately, I land what looks like a very good long term Career move with *Title Insurance and Trust Company (Ticor)* at age 36; until later events cause my retirement a year early in 1992, when I'm 64...after 28 years of service with *Ticor* which is sold after many years of less profitable results that resulted in smaller payments into the retirements funds: I recall Jay warning me of high risks which can mean long term reduced future payoffs, if any at all, because of too many uncontrollable events, especially those we have no control over, like prices in western real estate or bankruptcies. I also think, *of being talked into giving up my bank job in 1953 without knowing the impact of the cease fire in Korea which, in effect, ended the war, the, Phoenix employment market, and I move to California with no job.*

Fragment: Idea, Ice Cubes

I also recalled a series of conversations with my friend Lewis prior to his retirement party at his home in Simsbury, Connecticut, when Angie and I visited him to see the autumn leaves and he and I discussed his amplified view of the popular cultural concept of most trips many make to see the fall foliage in New England.

Lewis said, "I look beyond thinking of the leaves falling, changing colors, especially when they turn deep dark brown, they die, and it's nature's gift by furnishing organic fodder to also get ready for Spring and by being ready for new life which will begin when buds and green leaves show."

Then as an excuse for the retirement party, Lewis and I set out to buy all the ice cubes available in Simsbury; it was very obvious Lewis was doing a singular thing: he bought many more ice cubes than ever could be used by the bartenders to mix all the drinks possibly needed by even the thirstiest celebrants at his party. Lewis stored all the cubes in every storage site in his entire home: the kitchen, refrigerators in the garage, his study, spare bowls, pitchers and even extra glasses. Soon I wondered, *what's the hidden meaning of so many ice cubes might they be connected to the usual death symbol of decaying autumn leaves that Lewis also thought of as natural symbols for a new life in the coming Spring season.*

The next morning it was doubly clear to me: in our conversations, I realized that Lewis was not well, and he was hanging on to life like the sailor he was in WW II, and that the excess ice cubes would melt, change physical form, and become part of the water badly needed to nourish new growth. It was, as if, Lewis had visualized how his retirement party would be remembered by everyone as the party with a surprise ending...not as just a traditional cultural autumn leaves event, but that especially, Angie and I were ever so thankful we had made the trip; to see him most particularly; I was particularly pleased I had said goodbye to my best college friend and understood his conversation, its symbols, that he wanted me to appreciate and remember.

The idea Lewis advanced that autumn leaves mean both death and a new, next life, or as a separate set of double-word symbols imply, that *Sameness* to *Newness* occurs, but without any hint, as Lewis also believed and that few understood, that there is a missing part of the cycle that is called...*Satisfaction*...which energizes; especially, when old friends arrive and cause: trips to Boston, a great lunch, shopping, sight–seeing everywhere, and treasured goodbyes which create more memories to be added to the new three word cycle of *Sameness, Newness, Satisfaction* and where, in time, the collection of ice cubes can both begin and end.

Fragment: Funeral

The unusual event of connecting Fragments is also illustrated tellingly at a series of happenstances that began in March 2010 at the funeral of Dick Young, my nephew who was tragically injured in a sever accident that led to his death at age 56, by the *announcement* of a wedding to occur, more than a year in the future, in April 2011, but brought up during the funeral service for Dick. It was this very event that made me remember Lewis and his ice cube symbol.

In this situation, however, the 'death next life cycle,' in nature, had no reality to the final death phenomenon of the human funeral. The eager young man announcing his coming marriage should clearly have delayed his news to a more appropriate time when marriage happiness news could appropriately be received…not at a funeral.

The groom's father also was at fault by confidently predicting that Grandfather would not come to the Southern Georgia wedding based on his belief of financial negligence in the past of family financial responsibilities; this statement is all tragically incorrect: the connection between a funeral Fragment and a wedding Fragment was totally improper: The Grandfather had been supporting the family with thousands, of dollars over many, many years, to the extent that, in fact, too much financial support was available to the point it was taken for granted and always expected, and to a great extent resented, by his oldest son, who believes exactly what he says: Dad is rich and does not do enough; especially for me.

The *actual* reasons why Grandfather declined to come to the wedding were: the extended travel time, over 12 hours each way, his age, 83, financial assistance already in place or would have to be reduced or temporarily dropped, also the size of traditional wedding gifts Grandfather always gave. In truth, over many years Grandfather had shared what he could for his family; even paying for private schooling...as for his oldest son when needed.

Partial descriptions are as follows: major bankruptcy of oldest son caused by the charges he made to wife's credit card: in 1999-2002; medical costs for youngest son at Stanford University Medical, graduations gifts, presents for all three sons; Christmas gifts for everyone; when needed grandchildren room and board at colleges, over eight years; house projects for youngest son and other repairs, in years 98, 99, 2002...and as mentioned, wedding gift for sons and grandsons

Fragment: HMS Ferret

About a kilometer to the South, fishing fleet boat masts can be seen between the palms and mangrove trees. The masts described strange angles because the boats have been pulled up on the sand as fishing for the day is over and the fishermen are busy selling their catch to people from the commune and the nearby area. With heat, humidity and fish, the commune begins to smell; it will get worse as more people join the commune and the heat and humidity increase.

Pierre takes pictures and watches in a rather detached way all that is going on everywhere in the commune. He senses and then confirms a glimpse of a soft purple color moving between the trees. The color comes toward him. Soon, he sees the source; a young woman clad in a type of clothing he has never seen before. It fits her body like a swimming suit but is made from what appears to be soft, supple material. Every curve of her young body is visible and the effect of the material around her breasts is startling…it is like she is wearing a custom, expensive French bra that does what it was supposed to do but without any reshaping, just natural display.

Pierre tries not to stare but there is no way he can avoid looking at this wonderful beauty without staring; however, with his mission in mind he knows it is neither safe nor wise for him to lose attention to his surroundings. For some reason, he addresses the young lady in French, saying, *"bon matin"* …she says, *"also monsieur"* …but in excellent French. (*aussi, monsieur*). She smiles, not a self-conscious smile but a matter of fact, self-confident smile and leaves quickly disappearing beyond a small commune store that sells beer and supplies.

Pierre hears the tell-tale sound of an automatic pistol arming, slide and rolls instantly off the log where he is sitting…before he can do anything, though he has drawn his PPK Walther. He hears the unmistakable sound of an American Colt firing two rapid shots. Pierre, facing his front, sees the man who is ready to shoot him, is knocked backwards, the shot he does fire goes straight up in the air; another man, half hidden in the trees, is also knocked over but it's a head shot and he drops straight to the ground.

Pierre keeps right on rolling as he hit the sand and rolls on to his feet and runs for the parking lot and his Jeep. He hears the cough of a truck's diesel engine and the clack, clack of tappets. It will be a race for his life. The commune and the fishing village obviously are the collective/shopping/terminuses for the drug truck he was following. Every effort would now be made to keep him from sharing that information and the pictures he took. Pierre has no idea how many he faces or who has just saved his life. From the Colt sound, he knows it's an American, and a damn good shot too, just two shots!

The Jeep engine starts on the first try; at the same instant, Pierre activates the transponder concealed beneath the Jeep's dash...its emergency signal would be transmitted to a British frigate somewhere to the South off the coast of Belize. For Pierre, it is critical just how far away its location is. He figures the drug guys had been so confident of success with their attack on him at the beach that obviously neither the Jeep's engine nor its transponder had been disabled. At that moment Pierre hears two more rapid Colt shots followed by yet another two. He thinks, *I'll turn South at the 307 hoping the Drug Truck is going North along with the rest of the drug gang guessing that is the direction I'll be taking.*

On the Bridge, the Transponder

On the bridge of HMS *Ferret*, Commander Trevor Bryan is watching the late morning sun's position. He is startled by a sudden interruption by Ensign Franklin

"The Frenchman's transponder has just gone active, Sir, on the urgent, emergency channel. We've asked the American Orion aircraft if they can give us its longitude and latitude."

"Very good, Number One, bring everyone to alert status and ask the SAS team leader to report to me. Let me know, as well, the minute we have a fix on the position."

"Roger, Sir."

Commander Bryan disliked these waters: the long reef, lack of depth that rather makes navigation tricky and for all he currently knows, the *Ferret* could be headed in the wrong direction. *Hopefully,* he thought, *we are moving toward a man who is known for courage but, at this moment, needs our help in a very urgent way.* The Commander bends over the chart they are using now looking for openings in the reef between their location and possible reef opening, both to the North and to the South. Their charts, of course, are those made by the Royal Navy when Belize was British Honduras.

"You wished to see me, "Commander.""

"Yes, Major Gloster. We are receiving signals on the extreme urgency channel from the French Agent who is following the drug shipment north from Guatemala through Belize and on to an unknown destination somewhere in Mexico. I want your Royal Marines ready as you many have to go in and get him: probably using our tenders because of the reef.

"Very good, Commander, we'll be ready."

"Excuse me, Sir, the Americans now have a fix; the Frenchman has just turned south on 307 and the nearest pick up will be our point B."

"Thank you, Number One. What time is sunset today?"

"At 1830 hours, Sir, but it's just after 1200 hours now and by arrival time at Point B, we may be too late to help."

Special Forces

Pierre turned onto 307 when he saw exactly what he hoped for, a man flagging him to stop who had to be a member of American Special Forces. Pierre stopped.

"You will be safe from here, North or South, Sir, good luck. If you are going north, can you give me a ride to Cancun? My name is Jesse. No questions, please."

American Report

"News, Ensign?"

"Yes, Sir; The Americans report the French Agent is safe and now on his way to Cancun. The truck is in American hands and no former delivery personnel are available for reassignment."

Hook, Line, Sinker

Pierre sat on the beach in front of the Omni Cancun hotel where he met an American family in its lobby looking for someone to teach their infant son not to be afraid of the ocean; my job, holding Douglas above and toes in the small waves, is complete and Douglas is a new friend to whom I'm also teaching French…the first lesson is how to ask a person's name, *Comment vous appellez-vous.*

Suddenly a voice said, *"Je m'appell, Eloise."*

Pierre jumps up, turns, and there she is in a soft purple color Bikini. Pierre said, *"Bon Jour."*

And kisses her.

Eloise changing to English, said, "Good day, and please kiss me again. I never thought I would ever see you again after all the shooting at the Commune. I thought you had been shot because no one could remember you…!"

Pierre stops her talking by kissing her again, and said, "Are you staying at the Omni Cancun and would you like to have lunch?"

Yes

"Oh, of course, but in a different position; and as I said at lunch, I love tennis. And so does my best friend, Sally who is here in Cancun. When her husband is away, she always wants a good massage, too. She could join us; next time, pay more attention to my legs above the knees. Does that sound okay to you?"

"Absolutely, so, how do we plan this evening?"

"Would you like to see, again, the wonderful smock I was wearing at the Commune when you first saw me and wonder3ed what was under it besides me?"

"Can't wait…but first we should shower."

Eloise got out of bed, grabbed Pierre's hand so both went to shower. He soaped her all over, everywhere, rinsed her off and she got out of the shower to dry and dress. Eloise, naked, waited for him, got out of the smock, as she called it, slipped it over her head without putting on any underwear. Pierre experienced, once again, his view of her, all the curves, the effect of the soft material around her breasts and how she smiled at him when he said good morning; then she said, "I knew when I first saw you, you didn't have a chance."

"Neither did you," he said, "but you can't go out this evening, basically naked."

"So, why don't we call room service, order dinner, watch TV and you can help me out of my smock, hug and kiss me, and if all goes well, I can have another massage and Sally can wait until another time to join us…deal?"

"Of course, it sounds like a perfect solution to nakedness at a restaurant."

Breakfast

"Come on, dear, we should go down to get coffee, toast and discuss our plans. If you want, I can have my massage now or later. But really, we need to share information about our stay in Cancun and what happens next." Eloise said.

Pierre tells the waitress, "I'll have regular coffee and French toast. How about you, Eloise?"

"Sounds great, I'll have the same."

Demasquee

While eating, Pierre talks about being in Government Service…his assignment is for the rest of the week in Cancun, six more days, and then her returns to Paris for his next assignment. Eloise said she has the same time, type of schedule, lives near Paris and it would be fun, a real pleasure, to fly to Paris with him.

Taking turns, Eloise states what she want to do: shopping to get a couple of French summer dresses she saw in a window, regular underwear to match, to keep Pierre under control; takes the ferry to Cozumel, the island to the South, to see Mayan ruins, and sea floor plants turned to coral; skip Tulum, which was on yesterday's schedule; and also skip the Commune, dear, as you don't need to view any more naked, young women to compete with me; leave time to practice Spanish; also to eat every night at romantic restaurants that you pick out; and, of course, plenty of massages and showers."

"Sounds perfect, count me in on the whole program. I will have to make a single stop for information, tickets, money, and a firm flight schedule."

Eloise insists Pierre help pick out the colors of the dresses and underwear. He likes when she tried it on in the fitting room and especially the French Toulon Dressing Gown, she pretends is to wear to watch TV. They have so much fun with all their activities and about claiming they are making memories, right now, based on their experiences.

Paris

When they get off the plane at de Galle Airport in Paris, Eloise's parents are there to meet them. Her mother, Cynthia, knows immediately that her daughter has found *the right one*. She hugs Pierre with passion and said, "When?"

Eloise said, "Next week."

Cynthia said, "Did you buy Honeymoon clothes?"

"Of course, I even had Pierre view and approve all my purchases."

"Pierre says, "It's *Happenstance, I never had a chance.*"

Fragment: Getting a Date 1982 – Percy and Louise, A Novella

Commentary

I registered for the draft in July 1975 at 18. However, the war in Vietnam ended in April 1975 and drafting teenagers was over. I got a job several months later as a messenger for an insurance firm at 433 South Spring Street in Los Angeles: *Title Insurance and Trust Company*; I've worked for them for five years.

I speculated: *any chance of getting a date with one of their really good-looking young women in the legal office would be unlikely as these gals are only interested in moving up the financial ladder; I'm only a low paid messenger who's had several promotions over the years.* However, I'm still talking about night school, to anyone who will listen, about enrolling in legal classes at the USC downtown facility.

On my last interview with the enrollment people, I had a talk with a very smart USC dean who advised me to look into getting someone to move in with me and share expenses while I also look for promotion to another position than messenger and plan for a better future. He mentioned there is a new program starting where couples living together can file tax returns for both state and Federal purposes, called Considered Married, which obviously changes taxes due by both being in the Married payer category; it came about because California is a Common Law state, as are both Oregon and Washington. He advised me to investigate all this and tell a possible roommate I'm enrolling in night school law classes.

I'm thinking this all over when Louise Hodges, one of the most sought after gals any one could ever hope to get a date with, let alone allows you to hold her hand, joins me in the cafeteria, and said, "Do you still have a room at a small house on Bonita between Olympic and Pico on the bus line downtown to all the businesses on Spring Street?"

"Sure, I do, why do you ask?"

"I work at *O'Melveny & Myers*, I've lost my room near UCLA, at the last minute, and I'm wondering if you would let me stay with you for 9 days until I leave my job here and move to San Francisco for my new job. We can work out a plan for me to share rent, save my job here, and move to my new paralegal trainee job in San Francisco."

"Of course, Louise, but just call me, Percy; however, I have a very small room and sleeping for two can't be set up easily. Strangely, my land lady asked me the other day when was going to get a roommate, so, I know she will not object to whatever I would work out about rent to cover increased utility costs."

"I don't see any problem; we can just get acquainted. Can I move in tonight? I have to be out of my UCLA room first thing in the morning."

It all worked out beyond my wildest imagination; Louise was so relaxed she never hesitated to let me help her dress, (or undress, since she wears no night gown).And, first thing, in the morning, I fasten her Elegance, Full Style, Conturelle D Cup bra, when she decides to wear it, but her breast muscles sure didn't need any assistance. Also, she lets me pick out her camisoles, play any of her CDs so we can dress and undress to music; she mentions, too, she takes the pill, so I'm not to worry about that or her taking extra time to undress for bed or redress in the morning. All this turns out to be the happiest nine days in my life: and, of course, the most complex, surprising, unusual and exciting helping to fit Louise's breasts into her new bra cups when I'm needed. Moreover, to assist her to avoid pregnancy during our nine-day hookup adventure because she says she just wants to practice, at least once a day, while pretending she is only testing possible mates before pregnancy. It isn't until later that I learn that *O'Melveny & Myers* has a strict rule about unmarried employees living with the opposite sex while pretending to be married.

Louise Day 2

'Cause when the lovin' starts and lights go down…woo me up
till the sun comes up and you say that you love me…'
Say You Love Me, Fleetwood Mac, Keith Olson, 1977

Despite Louise's short time with me and what I learn about the law firm employment rules, I put the law school idea aside until I find out what is really happening at the Title Company; so, even if Louise and I are working for the same firm and violating rules about unmarried couples living together, I leave my messenger clerk assignment untouched. But, on my next quick Title Company trip, I meet with the supervisor of the Lot Book Department and ask a few questions about opportunities to learn that phase of the title business.

The supervisor gives me a strange look and says, "How old are you?"

"I'll be 26 in July."

"I'd advise you to stay at the law company until things calm down here. We got a new CEO in '82 and it looks like there are going to be changes; so, check back with me after your birthday, and we can talk about employment opportunities."

I agree and continue as is.

That evening I tell Louise what I learned; she said, "You got good information. We heard about big changes at the title company and that parts of the corporation are up for sale; so with this new information, why don't you go back to the USC Law School night classes idea as an interim answer until I leave in only a week now; just stay put and keep quiet about our living together adventure."

To get ready for bed, with her night gown off, I massage Louise in all her naked areas in a long nude all over massage; she returns the attention by giving me a quick gentle back rub for stress and friendship which she calls "getting acquainted". We both prolong the intimate touching and in only the correct, proper moments, we drop into bed and eventual sleep until the alarm goes off, which is when we begin what becomes our usual morning exercises.

At our lunch break, we decide to get more information on tax laws from the IRS about a new law for unmarried people living together, in community law states, which for tax purposes are now called: *Considered Married*. So, we decide to continue to say goodbye to each other for our last days together are over and we separate at the end of what Louise calls, *Our Adventure*.

Louise Day 3

With opportune invention, Time,
Enchanted, sat with us
Pausing amid her fragile
Selections, choices of variable feelings:
Passion, Acceptance,
Disenchantment,
Or Guile—.
But God, having given us free will,
Watched and waited
Waited, Waited,
And eventually retired.

Passion continues

Pride, Envy, and Avarice are the three sparks
that have set these hearts on fire.
The Divine Comedy, 1310-1321, Inferno, VI, L74 Dante Alighieri.

Louise Days 4-9

After Louise leaves, I read the advice in the poem, *Summa*; it seems good except it does caution that accomplishment is not simple, and that is where our tale continues. I decide only a complex venture could contain the four essential factors which he believes make attainment of a Leverage Buy-out difficult, maybe an impossible goal, the real test of achieving a designation of; *The Best Rating*: which is to seek after in evaluating a Leverage Buy-out. So, Bob searches financial newspapers sources to locate what is in play.

I locate coverage of a takeover still in progress that began in 1985. The target is an industry leading insurance company in a specialized part of the insurance industry; a little-known specialty activity called Title Insurance. I did more research among the financial publications and found, indeed, that the details of this buyout put the venture in the category of substantial success, but also *at substantial risk.*

I take more notes; the acquiring group would need to borrow substantial money from the usual variety of sources: bank loans, stock sales, short term secured notes and protracted long term payoff paper such as mortgages on real estate always subject to the sensitive market of real estate prices coupled with, of course, all the machinations of government, at all levels, with actions in play at any given time. Also, the acquiring group would face the need to sell the target's assets, if any, to raise money and reduce the amount of borrowed money—sale of assets, however, would impact the ability to raise money by the remaining Title Insurance company structure.

My Birthday in 1983

It is not necessary for me to wait until after my birthday to learn about events at the title Corporation; the papers which Louise brings home are full of the news about a big railroad company that owns the title company which it is selling it to an Investor Group that wants to buy it for $271.3 million in what is called a leverage buy-out transaction. This sounds like in order to pay for the buy, the Group, needs to sell part of the title company to raise cash to make the buyout work.

The LBO sale closes at the same time, parts of Ticor are sold: Home Realty, Life Insurance, and The Jeffries Print Network. The Trust Department is to be sold later.

Within weeks the papers are full of problems about companies that are selling Mortgage Insurance which pays when home buyers default on payments on part of their mortgage loans. One of the companies that sold the Mortgage Insurance policies, from whom the buyers bought policies in compliance with lender requirements that such insurance must be purchased in order to be qualified to get the home loan is Ticor.

The newspaper stories are quite complex but what is very clear is that Ticor's subsidiary that sells Mortgage Insurance coverage TMIC is in trouble. Percy and Louise not only read about all this, but Louise hears more news at work which she shares with Percy.

He said, "I'm glad I went to night school; I might have had a job at the Title Company where I'd be out of work now."

Fragment: Disaster, Warning, 1982

Introduction

Envy feeds on the living.
It ceases when they die...
Ovid quoted in Envy, a dictionary for the Jealous,
Adams Media, a division of F+W Media Inc.
Avon, MA 03022, U.S.A.

Eventually, the California Insurance Commissioner assumed daily control of the Ticor unit which had been renamed TMIC to be sure there was no confusion with the Ticor Title's Insurance subsidiary. The Commissioner halted any more sales of Mortgage insurance policies by TMIC which was established in 1981 and existed when the decision to do the leverage buy-out of Ticor, which closed in 1984. The debt-no-equity mess as a result of discounts, kickbacks, greed and the housing value collapse which impacted the issue of mortgage insurance policies that resulted in what I called a *Tar Baby*; because (TMIC) had by issuing mortgage insurance policies on what are now defaulted mortgages; moreover lenders demanded TMIC honor all its mortgage policies by paying on all policies it issued. *This led to the eventual bankruptcy of Ticor because, coupled with title insurance losses, which also drains resources to pay claims, it is obvious Ticor has to find a rich buy-out partner because Mortgage Insurance turns out to be a bad risk the title company cannot cover.* Even the government bureau Fannie Mae, with taxpayer money behind it, finds itself in a similar mess because it issued debt instruments called Derivative Mortgages, *smaller mortgages,* based upon the original, larger mortgage makings, generating monthly premium payments that are no longer are being paid. Therefore, the house of cards collapses when inadequate criteria governing lender rules for home purchasers became tragically obvious. The loss of jobs at the death of Ticor became significant.

Destruction, Fact, 1991

Conclusion

The ruin of Ticor was aided by top management which completely failed to understand the structure of the Title Insurance business: pricing of the entire product line sold by the Title Insurance company is based upon industry practice: loss avoidance, *not risk assumption*, which of course, is an *actuarial method of pricing* as in auto insurance, home owners insurance and umbrella type coverage often sold to cover high risk situations such as law suits or serious injury events, all of which are sold on the basis of actuarial random occurrences type pricing of monthly premium increase events covered by increased demands of customers who bought Mortgage insurance.

Bud, Definitions

Commentary

The business of title insurance is one of loss prevention not risk assumption; the tragedy of Ticor is that the last three CEOs: Johnny, Rocco, and Bud tried to change the business of Title Insurance into a system of risk, volume selling and ignoring loss while using the existing Title Insurance pricing concept that is based on a single, one time earned premium as the entire fee for the Title Insurance policy issued; this is industry practice. However, the creation of the Ticor Mortgage Insurance product line created pricing based on actuarial methods; with frequent premiums and normal risk assumptions for losses that occur in the future as random events. This resulted in Ticor's failure as the Title Insurance's part of Ticor couldn't cover TMIC losses as well as those now happening at the title company with its new risk pricing system.

Percy and Louise's Last Night Together

'Art is long, life is short, judgment
Difficult, opportunity transient.'
John W. Goethe, Wilhelm Meister's Apprenticeship.
1786-1820, ibid 9.

Percy said, "I guess we made the most of our short adventure by understanding Goethe; we are still together at my small rented room and Louise and I stayed at our mutual employer, *O'Melveny*, where Louise is now a paralegal assistant. I avoided Ticor Title Insurance, went to law school and will take the bar exam in a year; if I pass, maybe I can get a job offer at the new trust company downtown, called TSA, that Ticor sold to one of the big banks. However, for me, the tragic loss of jobs at Ticor Title does hurt; I used to deliver so much mail there, I got to know so many of the employees."

Louise listens quietly and said, "I feel very sad for the Ticor Title Insurance employees, male and female, who sure are *losing more than jobs,* they are losing longtime friends that amount to *their extended family* which they have had with their fellow employees with whom they worked for many years."

"True, Louise, but my conclusion, also, is that the former top management at Ticor couldn't care less about regular employees who lost what you just called, "extended family"; because the top younger people always had smaller salaries and will have less trouble finding new jobs at regular companies that pay lesser salaries, so why be over concerned. Just recall also, that normal risk assumption always includes possible losses and they often can occur in the future at random times; that is part of the fault of parent Ticor's failure to cover TMIC losses as well as those now happening in the Title company which has a traditional pricing structure that management changed; TMIC should have been junked except the lure of frequent monthly premiums from Mortgage Insurance was so great it fit the risk profile of the guys who were part of the 'Liquidate and Leave' insiders group run by Bud, the new CEO, at 6300 Wilshire."

Fragment: Vested Interest, Culture

Keith Clark Replaces Bob Long

Commentary

Any sudden change may strike at a vested interest because the change process appears to cause one group to believe the proposed shift creates losses for them; on the other hand, another group believes the change creates gains for both points of view or only gain for special, one-time-only interests. *Keith Clarke graduates high school in June 1948 and goes to work immediately while he is still attending night school and majoring in Accounting and English; his job is at Title Insurance and Trust Company. In 1950, he volunteers to serve in the Air Force in the Korean War; promptly in 1953 when the shooting ends and everyone is released, he returns to his job where he stays until a series of buy-outs, of various types and kinds, changes Title Insurance and Trust Company to Ticor; this is in 1982, and the arrival of Vince. Keith has many promotions and finds himself head of an entire unit called Administrative Services. However, by now, Keith concludes that the new management of Ticor has a philosophy Keith calls: Greed, Risk and Malice and Good-Bye.*

Stealing, Gross Revenue, Lust

Introduction

Gross Revenue cutting is the latest way for all levels of employment to steal money from Ticor; the leader of course is the head man who has the most sophisticated approach including Title offices he closes to sell their real estate also other standalone units of Title Insurance and Trust Company like: Jeffries Bank Note…printers of currency, bank notes and stamps for foreign countries; most of Administrative Services…an internal Title company unit of seven functions, which Bud believes he can out source with contracts at a profit; Title officers misquoting the Schedule of Fees and Charges; inventing special lower cost Cancellation Charges, incorrect use of the Short Term Rate, and discounts for favorite customers to earn points for bonus consideration from repeat customers and ignoring use of micro extra work charge opportunities in complex oil, railroad and shore line land title orders. Then there was just plain stealing when the chances occurred as in false mileage claims on out of town projects. As the greed philosophy spreads and reduces gross industry revenue which causes smaller units specializing in fragments of the title industry to enter the title insurance business, the most serious result is the loss of expertise in title work and the increase in the frequency of title insurance policy losses. Gone is the 'long tail,' a frequency of loss that is spread out over time, so loss is often not a critical budget item. Office closings and sales also include selling off equipment, like in the Print Shop, which eliminates employee pension accruals. Another activity opposite to income cutting was cost increases by use of company assets for personal gain: phone use, copying of personal documents for tax time, school applications and other personnel needs including for friends. In remote offices distant from corporate headquarters, a significant number of large frauds occurred which resulted in the hiring of a former Secret Service Agent and he was able to stop things as well as in the firings of the guilty. However, recovering the stolen money was not very successful. Agents issuing your title insurance policies require significant controls, too, especially when Kickbacks are part of the equation in any area.

Risk Rules/Options

Commentary

Keith knew Risk means hazard, possible peril and the chance of Disaster; so, the *greater* your risk, tempting Fate, the more probable is failure. For example, entering a new insurance field with which you are unfamiliar and that is so subject to events over which you have no control: like fluctuations of value...let alone sales, in the real estate market, such were predictable in the California, market like in the slump that happened in 1983; and, of course the higher the values of property as made by representatives of the lenders who want you to agree to the loans which you are choosing to insure as part of the mortgage size, against fraud or default; nor can you have any control over government policies, at many levels...for example, real property taxation rates. Nor do you have any control over purchasers who, at any given moment, may decide to walk away from either their mortgage payment or the extra loan payment on your mortgage insurance policy. Your unknowns require careful consideration and enormous capital reserves... for new capital donations, as are required to reduce risk for lenders as well; when there is no longer any equity protecting the loan debt.

Critical, examples repeated; the following is included for risk evaluation purposes by: Standard & Poor's, *in rating mortgage insurance companies, in its 1978, list:*

1. No more than 20% to 25% of a mortgage insurer's policy should be in any one state.
2. No more than 15% of its policies should be in one metropolitan area.
3. No more than 1% of its policies should be from any one institution.
4. No more than 2% of its policies should be in projects built by any single developer.

A factor as well is the decline in the quality of work at Ticor and a final death of an ancient myth that TI is as strong as Fort Knox, and will always survive; but what if, with mortgage insurance, the collapse of real estate values and there is no equity left in real property, as mentioned above, lenders demand capital payments on part or all of the insured mortgage amount and when TMIC collapses and the State Insurance Commissioner bans further issue of its policies. Ticor fails and is bankrupt.

> "...like a light love disappears
> But hearts are good for souvenirs
> And memories are forever..."

All This Time, Tim James & Steve McClintock, 1988

Fragment: Mom and Sissie – Recollections

Commentary

Mom and Sissie are not relatives but have near identical personalities which, among other characteristics, include adventuresome; expert shoppers; addiction to all sorts of social activities; adept at creating spontaneous informal fun-time events which always include bourbon highballs to stimulate outrageous outcomes. In short, Mom and Sissie are alter egos, counterparts of each other.

Sissie also has a small group of fun-loving 'Usual Suspects' that often tag along with her: that's Lucille and Tom and Florence and Karl. Meld these two sets of couples, Sissie, and her current companion with whom she is having fun and cause this entourage to gather at our house, and you have the correct chemistry. Correct, of course, means that Sissie, with her eclectic energy, plus that of the Usual Suspects, causes a special reaction to occur. Add that to the liveliness generated by Mom, and there is guaranteed major excitement.

So, I've assembled from my journals, six early year events which made Mom, Sissie's Usual Suspects, and others, burst into laughter as they embellished the retelling of each event with exaggeration, imagination that also included actual, appropriate sexual flavoring. I'm convinced these memorable happenings are milestones, which are key triggers for Mom, Sissie, and her small group, to highlight the passage of time. Another factor is that Sissie always brings roses for her visits. That's, Four Roses, and Sissie being in the financial business, (CPA), keeps timely, accurate records of purchases and consumption. Four Roses, by coincidence, is Mom's favorite Bourbon Blend. So, all told, Sissie's visits, the chemistry and the correct bourbon assisted in both the creation of outstanding events, and later, the enhanced recall process. A seventh special event did occur, and it is also included.

Introduction

The Great Highball and Thanksgiving Turkey Cook-a-Thon Event 1

One of the cardinal rules, at our house, in those early memorable days was the ritual surrounding cooking. Put bluntly my Grandmother, Annie, did the holiday cooking; except when Mom, Sissie and the *Usual Suspects*, were present. Then, anything *could* happen and *did*. So, when the entourage got out the highball glasses, soda water and ice from the refrigerator, and removed the bottle(s) of *Four Roses* from the liquor-store bag, Annie left the kitchen in haste and retreated to her room upstairs. It was a fact that serious chemistry and the number of highball participants, in excess of two, always dictated more than one bottle of *Four Roses* was required.

About 12:30 pm that eventual Thursday, after Tom was named bartender and Sissie's companion, Frank, an assistant, and the first round of highballs of bourbon and soda were mixed and served, Mom, Sissie, Florence, Lucille and Karl, with drinks in hand, adjourned to the nearby living room. It was there the supervisors, Mom and Sissie, planned, made work assignments and issued instructions for the entire sequence of dinner preparation steps.

A key instruction was to reduce crowding in the kitchen. So, when not executing your dinner assignment, each member of the team was directed to return to the living room, to relax and to continue highball consumption. (Note: highball drinking is an activity which occurs whenever and wherever any of the participants are located: kitchen, dining room, living room, etc.).

The plan and sequence of events, as I recall: first, my sister, Kelly, and I were to set the table with places for ten. We were told to leave one place empty. We put out dinner plates, water glasses, silverware, napkins, coffee cups, and so forth. Obviously, Grandmother was miffed and was not eating with us.

Second, Mom announced all dinner food preparation assignments: "Lucille, potatoes: bake sweet potatoes with brown sugar/marshmallows and boil regular potatoes, mash with butter. Florence, vegetables: cooked carrots and peas, seasoned, cut and dice celery for the stuffing, and heat dinner rolls. Sissie, stuffing: boil chestnuts, peel and dice them, slit a Bermuda onion, dice, and sauté it in butter and slice additional butter to melt later for the stuffing. Karl, stuffing: lightly toast and dice bread, get prepared chestnuts from Sissie and celery from Florence, get a bowl and mix everything for the stuffing. Mom, melt more butter and pour it into the ingredients for the stuffing, mix and with Sissie's help at the right time, stuff the turkey; put on the table in small dishes the cranberry sauce, olives and celery; take pies from the refrigerator to be heated later for dessert."

Once again, Sissie urged all participants, "When waiting to finish your assignment or after work is completed, go to the living room, relax and continue to enjoy your highballs. If you need refills tell Tom or Frank."

'I knew dinner was set for around six, it was 1:30 and time for Mom and Sissie to stuff the turkey and get it in the oven or it would be too late to eat it today. Finally, my informal but highly accurate count placed all the participants, especially the ladies, ready for their third, maybe for some a fourth, highball. (Note: it became clear, as later confirmed, that Karl was not familiar with the instruction: "lightly toast" the bread for the stuffing…it was burned.) The result of this phase of The Great Highball and Thanksgiving Turkey Cook-a-Thon was that, "no pain Mom and Sissie", unconsciously stuffed the turkey with burned bread. The bird went into the oven around 1:45PM, and I went upstairs to my room to wait for dinner. About 3:15 a smell of burned bread drifted up to me on the second floor via the back stair-well from the kitchen and even on up to the attic.

Just then, I heard grandmother open her door and go down the back stairs to the kitchen. I followed quietly and watched Annie remove a large ham from the old ice box on the small, back porch beyond the main kitchen. She rubbed the ham with butter, sprinkled it with brown sugar and plugged some kind of dark things that looked like pins in it, put the ham in a roaster pan, started the old stove on the back porch and put the ham in the oven.

None of the Sissie crowd nor Mom saw or heard Grandmother or what she was doing. Nor did they notice the aroma of the baking ham as it cooked because the burned-bread-turkey smell covered it. At six the well-oiled Highball crowd carved the turkey and served it and all the fixings; the entire turkey, including the stuffing, were ruined and not edible. The taste of burned bread had permeated, flavored the entire bird and stuffing. By now, even the veteran Highball drinkers could taste the burned bread turkey; they realized there was a major problem. Sissie and Mom both broke into laughter. Mom said, "So, we eat sweet potatoes, mashed potatoes, carrots and peas, celery, olives, cranberry sauce and dinner rolls with pumpkin or mince pie for dessert."

But, at that very moment Grandmother came in carrying a large platter with a baked ham, and a carving knife and fork. She said in a very firm voice, "There is **no** exception to one of our cardinal rules. Annie does all the cooking on holidays."

Everyone applauded and cheered. Especially when Annie brought in the pies and coffee, took the tenth seat, and ate dinner with us. Later, she wanted to know who made the two kinds of potatoes. She said, "Not bad, must have used my recipes."

The Episode of the 50 Dollar Bill, Event 2

The time between Thanksgiving and Christmas passed quickly by retelling turkey dinner highlights, eating ham sandwiches, Mom having highballs and all of us enjoying Grandmother's Christmas Eve dinner.

Christmas Day, we kids opened presents. My sister hit the jackpot: two warm, acceptable style sweaters for school to go with her new wool skirt, a winter coat and a pair of boots to wear over regular shoes; all items required as snow was falling every day; the slushy residue was piled onto the sidewalks by the street sweepers making warm clothes and boots essential.

I got a pair of badly needed winter pants; my California stuff didn't cut it in Pennsylvania. I was trying them on, perfect fit, when around 9:30 am the phone rang. It was Aunt Sissie wanting to speak to Mom. Sissie isn't really our Aunt, we kids just call her that because she is always here which makes it seem like she is a relative. I said, "Sissie, Mom's not here, she's gone out with Harry Riley."

Aunt Sissie explained she's planning a shopping trip to *J. Pross*, the best boutique in town, for their after Christmas sale; her trip's scheduled for January 2nd because *J. Pross* is closed for the week between Christmas and New Year's. She also plans to include lunch at *The Tea Room* in the trip. I'm to give all this information to my Mom and if the timing is right, let me know, and tell her I'll stop by and get her at 10:00 am on the 2nd. Aunt Sissie added she got a bunch of money for Christmas and is ready to do some serious shopping. Sissie knew I'd report the money information to Mom who always has money for shopping, especially for girls. Those two facts, money and shopping for girls, made Sissie's plan as good as a done deal!

A Message, Event 3

Sissie's detailed, precise message was delivered to Mom at 11:00 am, especially including the part about Aunt Sissie getting money at Christmas and ready for serious shopping. Mom called back immediately, and I could hear her check out every detail of Aunt Sissie's shopping trip message. (Be aware, Mom is just like Adam's wife Eve...the world's first verifier); shopping, money and lunch were confirmed, the whole deal was set.

Time passed quickly, Event 4

Approximately at noon, however, disaster struck. Mom was yelling from upstairs for **everyone** to come to her room immediately; **everyone** meant: my sister, me and Grandmother. When we were all assembled (it took some time as Annie was in the basement doing wash), Mom stared at us obviously quite upset. She announced, "My Fifty-dollar bill is missing. I put it on the table by my bed."

Mom immediately questioned, "Who has been in my bedroom?" Since each of us could only answer for our self, the responses were direct and simple: Grandmother, "not me," "me, "Not me," my sister, "Yes, I have been, every day after school when you ask me to come in and share information with you about the events of the day." As to speculation about any others who might have been in Mom's bedroom, that was not a wise topic to pursue.

From that moment on, the most extensive search ever conducted of the four floors (basement to attic) of my Grandmother's house, **except** Mom's bedroom, began. Because, especially for me, we had no idea of where to look for a 50-dollar bill. Mom supervised the process from the outset. After the first hours on day one, I became the most disliked member of the search team. That was the result of what I said and repeated on every possible occasion, "It's a pity Sherlock Holmes isn't here as with his particular skills of starting at the end of a puzzle and working backward to the onset, he would soon locate the missing object and solve the whole problem."

Holmes, of course was not available to solve everything so an attitude called 'mounting suspicions' began. First, by Mom insisting that one of us knew where the money was, second, as a result of the searches producing nothing and third, as the hours and days passed and no 50 dollars for shopping was found. Not only did the attitude of 'mounting suspicions' increase but it prospered and soon had a life of its own separate from finding the 50-dollar bill. In particular, tension increased when Mom started to drink highballs to ease the stress. I began to say to myself that Mom had what I called, *Highball-itis*.

By day six, December 30th, there was no 50-dollar bill. Worse yet, it was only 3 days to Aunt Sissie's shopping trip. Mom had to have the 50 dollars to go on the trip since I heard her tell Grandmother that the monthly check from the trust for the kids never arrives until the end of the first week of each month. And it was precisely after Mom gave that information to Grandmother that once again, I brought up my Sherlock Holmes observation.

Mom said, "You mention Sherlock Holmes one more time, and I will return your winter trousers to *Rogers* and use the money for my shopping trip with Sissie." I stopped.

Another problem surfaced and was brought to our attention: tomorrow is December 31st and its New Year's Eve. Mom is going out to dinner and dancing at the Country Club with Harry Riley. She will need time to dress, etc. and will not be able to supervise the search team during its final, critical hours.

Dinner, Dancing, Event 5

Mom and Harry Riley left for dinner and dancing at the Country Club. It was then I said to Grandmother, "Maybe we need to change the premise that the missing 50-dollar bill is somewhere else in the house but it's in Mom's bedroom which we never are allowed to search?" Grandmother agreed.

The whole team went to the second floor, straight across the narrow hall to the door to Mom's bedroom and boldly entered. Work was divided by Grandmother. She checked all the purses; my sister the dresser drawers including underwear; and using the Holmes approach, I was assigned to search the table by the bed which was the last known location of the 50-dollar bill. The first thing I did was pick up the book Mom said she was reading, turn it upside down and fan all the pages. Everyone watched the 50-dollar bill fall out and drop to the floor...it was used as a bookmark. Grandmother took charge of the money to give to Mom in the morning, January first.

Joy, Event 6

Filled with joy, all the members of the search team met in front of Mom's door on New Years' Day, we knocked. Mom greeted us with the results of the aftermath of too many highballs the night before. Grandmother handed Mom the 50-dollar bill and said, "It was found in the book you were reading that was on the table next to your bed; the money evidently was used by you as a bookmark."

Relief, Event 7

Mom was relieved, but not satisfied; happy with the solution. She said, "So, one of you planted it there while I was away last evening! This act of stealing is not solved; it is fact that one of you is guilty I have a headache; I'll be down for coffee later."

`Mom's 35th Birthday, Event 8

Sissie met with Grandmother, Kelly and me to plan a surprise birthday for Mom on the 20th of February. The idea was an early afternoon cake and ice cream party for five of us. Sissie said, "Mom will be going out to dinner with Harry Riley. There is a chance, however, that Harry might invite me and my special friends to join them. So, an early party for Mom with just the five of us is definitely needed."

Annie said, "I can make a round, double layer white cake with chocolate icing, at the store get some French Vanilla ice cream and flavored sprinkles to put on the ice cream, have coffee for myself, Sissie and Mom, and chocolate milk for Kelly and Cole."

Everyone agreed that the food plan for the party was great. Then, the question about birthday gifts came up and both Grandmother and Sissie suggested a card would be the best solution. Sissie volunteered to bring one with her and we could all sign it and put it on the table next to the cake. I said nothing, but *really liked the card idea for a present as neither of us, Kelly nor me, had any allowance money; and I only made a dime from my magazine route.*

Grandmother said, "I'll get Mom to agree to a time even though I have to spoil the surprise part because if she is going out with Harry, there is no way we can guess what time will be right and my daughter is not keen on times she did not agree to."

Sunday, the 20th, Event 9

Sunday morning of the 20th Mom was in a really good mood. I heard her tell Grandmother she is going out to a birthday dinner with Harry and he's invited Sissie and her *Usual Suspects* to join us. We are going to the Mountain View Inn and that Harry has a big surprise planned. Then, to start the evening out on the right foot, everyone is meeting here for drinks, bourbon highballs, at 5 pm; dinner reservations are at 6:30 pm.

I heard Grandmother and Mom talking, "Sissie and the kids have a surprise cake, ice cream and coffee party planned for you at about 2:00 PM. Does that leave plenty of time for you to be ready for drinks at five?"

"Two is late. Can the cake and ice cream party be moved to 1:30 or 1:00?" Mom said.

"Which time is really better?"

"I'd like 1:00 better so I can relax, dress and be ready by 5. Not to disappoint Kelly and Cole, but the cake party should be over by 1:30."

"Sure, that's easy; I'll call Sissie and take care of all the other details. I'll bake the cake this morning, get all the other food at the store and be ready at 1:00 PM sharp. Do Sissie and her friends know about being here at five for cocktails?"

"Of course, Harry and I have taken care of everything."

A Quick Birthday, Event 10

'Five of us sat in the dinning-room at 1 PM and waited. Mom arrived at 1:15, had coffee, a taste of cake, read the birthday card and left...just before 1:30. Sissie thanked us for the party, drank some coffee while Kelly and I ate cake and ice cream. Sissie pretended not to see our disappointment at the failed birthday surprise party. At 1:30 when the clock in the living room struck again on the half hour, just as it does on the hour, Sissie let us know she had to be on the way home, run errands and be ready for the highball party at 5:00 pm. So, Sissie stayed a little longer to please us and left about 1:45.

Sissie and the *Usual Suspects* arrived right at 5:00 bringing a renewed supply of roses, *Four Roses*. Mom was there to greet her guests, appoint Tom bartender, without an assistant, and thank each person for bringing a birthday gift.

Kelly and I sat on the stair landing which is the half-way point where the stairs turn to go the rest of way to the second floor; we watched everything. Kelly wanted to see what the women were wearing and commented on what she liked and didn't like. I watched the growing pile of gifts and by the size of the boxes tried to guess what was inside.

Harry Riley came at 5:15 and then the party really began to role. Tom was refilling highballs at a rapid rate, making sure everyone had a fresh drink. He strolled to the piano in the small music area next to the living room and played Happy Birthday. The singing was loud, off key and by 6:00 pm it was time to for the whole gang to leave for The Mountain View Inn.

Tom played a final sing-along of Happy Birthday which was really more a tribute to the power of highballs by *Four Roses*, Tom's bartender abilities than Mom's 35th birthday.

I wished I could be a witness at the dinner party and learn about Harry Riley's big surprise. I bet the next time Sissie comes over and she and Mom talk, I'll be able to hear all about it.

The Anderson Estate Sale, Event 11

Mom and Sissie were talking while sitting on the front porch on the side with the two rocking chairs. It was early April, the rains were about over, all the trees were leafing-out and the flowers along each side of the house all the way into the backyard were in bloom. The temperature was in the mid-70s; the weather perfect.

Kelly and I were on the swing on the opposite side of the porch, but we could hear what the two fast friends were talking about. Sissie was saying to Mom, "Are you still telling Harry 'No' to his surprise marriage proposal at your birthday party?"

Soon their conversation went back and forth: "It wasn't an emphatic, no; I sort of left the door ajar a little bit."

"But, does he see your response the same way you just described it?"

"He must as he still calls me; we went to the Country Club for the Valentine's Day Dance, spent some-time together in mid-March, and he is coming by later today to take us to the Anderson Estate Sale at the main Fire Station."

"Do I understand what you infer by '*some-time* together?"

"Of course, you do. Are you still seeing, Frank, our assistant bartender?"

"Only now and again," Sissie said. "He's been very busy at his job in Pittsburgh."

"How *much* of him does *now and again* mean?" Mom said.

"Probably the same as in *some-time together*. So, Riley is out? Do you think you can find someone else here?"

"Probably not, but, in Southern California, especially Los Angeles; it's a big community with lots of possibilities in the movie industry, oil, aircraft, shipping and the like. More than that, it's fun, fun, fun from all the social time at the big hotels, great restaurants and the nearby beach towns in the South Bay."

"Do you want to move back?"

"I'm thinking about it. It's too dull here."

"What about the kids? Here your mother runs the house: laundry, grocery shopping, cooking all the meals, looks out for the kids...she does everything."

"Right, but Kelly is in high school now and Cole will be next year in September. They can get lunch at the high school cafeteria and for dinner they are smart enough to stop at any of the cafes on Wilshire Boulevard after they get off the school bus on nights when I'm not at home cooking."

"You mean almost every night?'

"Of course, and that includes weekends when I leave Kelly in charge. I'll have it all planned out once I'm back in Los Angeles *playing the field*."

"That, of course, means male companionship."

"Yes, and with the Trusts paying all costs to run the house, money for the kids' clothes, meals out, the *whole ball game*, I don't have to worry."

"But time passes quickly, how long do the Trusts cover everything?"

"It's all set until Kelly and Cole are both 21 and/or out of College."

"So, you are looking at seven to eight years, but when the kids are away in college the Trusts aren't paying you, right? What about then?"

"I'll worry about that when the time comes."

"From your questions, Sissie, you sound a bit down."

"Yes, I've been thinking that we are concentrating only on what we are doing now, day to day, like parties, shopping, out to dinner dates, *Four Roses* fun times; really, no long-term objectives...plans."

"Sure, we look long range, Sissie. We both want a situation with a lover, maybe a mate, who's wealthy and can afford to give us the carefree, prosperous life we want."

"Are we that obvious?"

"Sure, we are. This is what I mean, what I'm saying, Sissie. For me, I need to locate the next man with enough money to take over. I don't think I will find him here. And I'm in the position that he won't have to pay any costs for the kids as the Trusts take care of that."

"What about any money left in the Trusts?"

"Well I'm doing my best to avoid that but if there is anything left, it goes to each one of them."

I was trying to understand what Mom and Sissie were saying about everything: child costs, money for us, when Kelly, who appeared to be only concerned with one of Mom's fashion magazines and not with what Sissie and Mom were saying, said, "What did Mom mean about money and looking for a man who had money? One who could give her a prosperous, carefree life?"

As I worried about what Kelly said I thought *this thing over money may mean bad things are going to happen…like how Mom acted and claimed one of us had taken her 50 dollar bill and some day she would find out who did it and get even with that person*; then Harry Riley drove up, parked in front of the house, got out of the car and said, "You ladies want to go to the Anderson Estate sale?"

"What and where is that, Harry?" Sissie said.

"It's part of the Estate liquidation of Anderson possessions from their expensive, large home over in West Greensburg near the Country Club. Some of the contents were moved to the main Fire Station on Pennsylvania Avenue, opposite the Penn Albert hotel and bar, where the sale is going to take place late this afternoon and early evening. There will be free food and a cash bar. The kids will be able to attend as the buffet will be separate from the bar. The buffet, of course, will take the place of cooking dinner. You gals really should come there will be music, too. All the fire houses, by Ward, held a competition to play at the sale and Fifth Ward won. So, some of the guys you know will be playing. They are part of the 'Fifth Ward Five'; they specialize in smooth, dance music from the Big Band era…like Artie Shaw's stuff."

"You're a great salesman, Harry, sounds good; Sissie, want to go?" Mom said.

"Sure, I'll go but first, I'll call Tom and Lucille, Florence and Karl and they can either meet us at the Fire Station or come here and have a small introductory party. Does everyone agree to a warm-up?" Sissie said.

"That's a perfect idea. I have enough *Four Roses* on hand to get us started, Sissie; what about Frank?"

"He's not in Pittsburgh today, away on a business trip," Sissie said.

"Good, you can all ride with me and, of course, your friends, Sissie, will have their own car," Harry said.

"I'll change while you're making your call, Sissie."

"No need to change to go to an Estate sale at a Fire Station. You gals look great in summer dresses; but, what about Annie coming along to watch the kids?" Harry said.

"The kids will be fine, and I doubt my mother wants to miss her late afternoon radio programs."

Four Roses, Event 12

I figured the *Four Roses* group would end the introductory highball party while the chauffeurs were still able to drive and five of us would pile into Harry Riley's car and the four *Usual Suspects* into Tom's car.

At the Fire House, Kelly and I headed for the buffet and the adults dropped anchor at the Cash Bar. The entire event as reported in the *Morning Review* became known as *The Famous Anderson Estate Sale*, because it evolved into more than a sale. It was an out-an-out drinking party based on an unusual rhythm connected to the frequency of purchase of estate items. The particular frequency I noted set an immediate tempo: one highball for each drawing or etching bought. The Andersons I determined must have had a passion to own the best collection of the finest academy drawings and etchings west of New York City. Mom and Sissie, Lucille and Florence ran out of money but ended the buying spree with the purchase of some very fine Kensington Ware serving platters, made right here in Westmoreland County, and some souvenir plates: such as the 1893 World's Columbian Exposition in Chicago, a Niagara Falls Honeymoon plate and a World War I US Army plate from the Fort Indiantown Gap infantry training facility. The Cash Bar sent out for more liquor from the Penn Albert Bar across the street, therefore, the Cash Bar must have raised more money than the sale did.

We filled the trunk of Harry Riley's car with purchases as we did Tom's car. Grandmother still has many of the drawings and etchings; ones that were unsuccessful resale items at subsequent sales.

Mom also bought some older, inexpensive books for Christmas...the one for me was a dictionary which I still have. It turned out to be a gem because it had extensive tables of the 1940 census by state and for all cities with populations over 1,300.

After the Cash Bar closed at 8 PM and the Estate sale was over, Mom, Sissie, Lucille and Florence decided it would be more fun to don fire helmets and jackets, climb onto one of the fire trucks, blow the horn and ring the bell. All were wearing short summer dresses, so the gals became immediate favorites with the crew of firemen on standby should they be needed to reply to any emergency.

The 'Fifth Ward Five', which had been playing at a moderate volume during the sale, the continuous drinking and expeditions to acquire more liquor, decided it was about to wrap things up but Mom persuaded the FWF to liven things up with some up-best arrangements by Miller, Kenton, Goodman and Shaw. Mom picked out one of the bachelors from the Fifth Ward she knew, grabbed him and started to dance. The rest of the firemen began dancing with all the women still at the fire house and the party rolled until near 10 pm when the Fire Captain broke it up.

As a fitting finish, Mom and Sissie, with music by the Fifth Ward Five, did a suggestive dance to the *Stripper*. Then Mom, Sissie, the *Usual Suspects* and the rest of us all headed home for a night-cap that Mom and Sissie suggested since it was too early to call it an evening and end the party; also, maybe everyone wanted to talk about the sale and to add a new event to their list of memorable events.

Idlewild Park, Event 13

Each year the school systems around Greensburg have picnics at Idlewild Park at the end of classes before summer recess begins. There is a spur rail line from the main line of the Pennsylvania Railroad at Greensburg to Idlewild and special trains take all the kids and their chaperons and teachers to the park. Idlewild is also accessible from highway 30 and many drives to the park, which is open all summer, for picnics and use of Park attractions, which includes a roller coaster. It's a small one, not like the one at Kennywood Park in Pittsburgh, but still great fun.

This year Greensburg's picnic day is Saturday, June 12, which is one week after my birthday on the 5th. So, Mom, Sissie and the *Usual Suspects* planned to combine both my birthday and the end of school with the summer celebration at Idlewild Park.

Mom, Sissie and Kelly, who insisted the school picnic was not for high school students, rode in Harry Riley's car with the picnic baskets; the Usual Suspects came in Tom's car. Grand-mother and I went by train. What boy would miss a ride on the train?

Alcohol is not allowed in the park, but the *Four Roses* group devised a strategy to disguise their 'beverages' and the fun was on. The train arrived around 10:30 when the park opened. Grandmother and I found Mom, Sissie and our table while all the kids on the train took off to see the Park attractions. Then, I lined up at the roller coaster where there was a long wait to get on, so it was at least a half hour after your first ride to pay 10 cents for another ride. Soon, the line was shorter as everyone had only enough money for maybe two or three rides.

I went back to the picnic table about noon for food. We had everything possible to eat, the list is too long to mention, and Grandmother even made apple pies for dessert. We had real plates, forks, spoons, knives and glasses for lemonade. The coffee the adults drank smelled a bit different to me, but I decided not to do my Sherlock Holmes impersonation after a stern look from Mom who was always able to guess what I was up to.

By 4 pm the train was ready to go back to the station in Greensburg, the coffee was all gone, and Mom, Sissie, Lucille and Florence could no longer see the softball in the girl's game they were trying to play; so, we all went home. Grandmother cleaned up the picnic stuff and put the baskets in Harry's car. She rode the train with me.

We walked home from the station and found the *Four Roses* group had decided they would have an early party as it was too early to call it a day because coffee and bourbon tend to nullify each other. Mom had changed to lounging pajamas, complete with Mom's favorite pink, bunny rabbit slippers, and she had started a coal fire in the fireplace grate in the living room 'to take the chill off' the living room.

The party was going full blast, so, Grandmother took the picnic baskets to the kitchen to clean up the plates and everything else. At that moment, a large lump of soft coal fell off the top of the coal pile in the grate and rolled beyond the hearth on to the rug. Mom kicked at it and her right, pink rabbit slipper flew off and onto the top of the fire in the grate. Everyone, but Mom of course, roared with laughter and shouted in unison, "Bet you can't do that again with the other slipper!"

Mom yelled, "It's not funny, everyone, the party is over, and you kids go to bed right now." Kelly and I scrammed up the stairs; it was lucky I left, as I was about to say, "We learned in General Science today that something, just like a slipper, is a *body*, and once that *body* is in motion, it stays in motion until something stops it. I figured I could use Mom's slipper as an illustration next week in class."

More? Event 14

After Sissie and the gang left, I heard Mom and Grandmother talking. So, I snuck out of my room and sat in my favorite hideaway spot which is on the stairs beyond the small landing where the next set of stairs turns to go the rest of the way to the second floor. You can hear anything in the living room but not be seen.

Grandmother was asking Mom about more money to run the house since all of us came from California. Mom was making jokes about how often she was out with Sissie or on a date so there was plenty of money for food just for the kids.

But Grandmother talked about food for parties and picnics and how often all of Mom's friends stop by and something called utilities being higher, too, and property taxes going up as well. Mom joked again saying she would shower with her dates at their houses and cut down on hot water and gas.

"That's not clever. Since my husband, Robert, died, I've had a real struggle and am convinced I have to sell this house and move back to Ligonier. It's less expensive there than Greensburg. The house in Ligonier is empty now, too, so I have no rent money coming in. I could use the money I sell this house for to make life easier for me. I still get a monthly payment from the insurance company and, of course, before you all arrived, I rented out your bedrooms to the girls who work at the phone company," Grandmother said.

"That's a good idea, and we can go back to California. My house is also available; but you can sell both your houses and come with us. It would be ideal for the kids to be with you, just like here, daily and you would not have the expenses like you just mentioned...the kid's trusts would take care of them."

"That's not a good idea for me. My whole life is here."

"Well, think it over. I'll go ahead with my plans to go back to California now that school for this year is over. Kelly will be a high school sophomore next year, and Cole will be a freshman. So, I see no problems about their changing schools."

I thought *here we go again, I won't tell Kelly, she's just made friends and will be upset. Wait to see what happens, Mom changes her mind all the time.* I went up to my bedroom before Mom and Grandmother came up stairs and caught me.

California and Christmas, Event 15

The trip to California in mid-August was lots of fun. Sissie decided to go with us to help Mom drive; to see our house in Holly-Woodland; and to turn the trip into another adventure. She stayed a month until we took her to Union Station to get the train to Pennsylvania; a tearful departure. However, before leaving, Sissie shopped Hollywood Boulevard and Rodeo Drive in Beverly Hills; drove to see: The Palladium, the Coconut Grove and the Troubadour. After that, all of us toured the Beach Cities in the South Bay; we kids went swimming by the Pier in Hermosa Beach...Mom and Sissie visited favorite 'watering holes' every afternoon and evening. Sissie said over and over, "Maybe I can come for Christmas, if I'm invited." Kelly and I missed her so much after she left on the train and, of course, begged Mom to invite her for Christmas."

In Mid-September we registered at Hollywood High. Once there we settled into a pattern of some cereal for breakfast, regular lunch at the H.S. Cafeteria and whatever Mom's instructions were for dinner. I had a class schedule of: Algebra I, General Science at the high school level, English, Latin and gym.

I began to lose track of Kelly; she made friends quickly and ate lunch with them and often one of her new friends would ask her for dinner. Mom was gone almost every day after school and into the evening, so, generally, I walked home from school and either got a hamburger at one of the HS kids favorite eating spots or ate leftovers out of our refrigerator. By Thanksgiving, it was getting to be a lonely life, and I realized how much I missed Grandmother. She sent me a letter with her new address on Main Street in Ligonier, told me where she walked to market, and that she made friends with a lady, Loda Blyth, who lived next door and was also a widow. I guessed Grandmother was lonely, too.

By the week before Christmas, everything changed. Sissie and Frank both arrived; we met them at Union Station near Olvera Street in Los Angeles…had a great tour of Mexican art and souvenirs, bought candles for Christmas and headed home.

Soon it was almost like old times. Mom had daily parties; Sissie got the *Four Roses* for a new bourbon crowd but the *Usual Suspects* were not there nor was Grandmother. We went shopping for a Christmas tree with one of Mom's boyfriends, Basil, an English guy from London who was a diplomat and part of the staff at the Consul in Los Angeles. Basil had a big pickup, so we were able to buy the largest tree possible that would fit in the living room.

Basil and two of his friends came to our Christmas party. He brought *Four Roses* for Mom, Sissie and Frank, the Bourbon Group, and *Bombay Gin* for himself and his two English friends, Percy and Edmund. Mom had all the boxes of ornaments ready, so, after drinks and snacks, everyone helped trim the tree. Mom, Sissie, Frank, Kelly and I did the tinsel and ornament hanging on the lower and middle branches. Basil and his tall friends, Percy and Edmund, did the upper branches we could not reach. For the adults I noticed that a definite rhythm had developed, string tinsel, hang ornaments…Stop, refresh yourself…*Four Roses* or *Bombay Gin*. It was really a big tree and before I was aware, there was more refreshment being consumed than decorating accomplished. Finally, however, the boxes of decorations were empty as well as the supply of liquor. Basil asked one of his friends, Percy, to fetch some inventory…as he described it…while everyone was relaxing.

That was when Mom started to finish the tree to her satisfaction by carefully hanging silver strips of flexible material on tree branches to simulate icicles. Kelly and I began to help as Percy returned and Basil and Frank began to mix new drinks. Of course, we could not reach the higher branches, neither could Mom. So, she began to toss the icicles at the higher branches and once again, a new rhythm began: toss sliver strips, sip a drink, toss silver strips, sip a drink; Basil and Frank began to lag a bit behind in the process called, 'freshen-up-your-drink' and at the same time the accuracy in tossing silver strip icicles at branches declined significantly; especially by the two females.

Basil and Frank began to aid the gal's tossing motions by standing behind them to guide their arms which, obviously, required a certain amount of physical touching. As soon…that's immediately, as the touching began, Percy and Edmund left, and Kelly and I went upstairs.'

"Bartender", Event 16

Early in June when it was warmer, four of us: Mom, Basil, Kelly and I went to Hermosa Beach to hear one of the famous WW II bands perform at a combination restaurant and bar at a location right before the Pier on Pier Avenue. The trip was so I could hear Freddie Slack. Kelly and I were not permitted in the bar, entertainment area, but we could sit in the waiting area next to the restaurant and hear everything.

Mom and Basil were sitting at the bar, their backs to me, but I easily saw them. The band didn't start to play until around 7 PM; we arrived some-time before 6:30, so, the drinking was underway a good half hour before any music. Without any noise, it was clear every time Basil called loudly, "Bartender, two more "Boor-bons and soda" Basil did not pronounce Bourbon correctly, but Mom had converted him from gin and now he could sure consume Bourbon. So, as it turned out, I was able to hear at least three or four additional calls of, "Bartender, two more Boor-bons and soda."

The Band began and somewhere around 7:30 Basil shortened his call to, "Bartender, two more." Which at 8:00 changed again to, "Bartender," and two fingers lifted. At 8:30 the means of communication changed to simply two fingers lifted.

Kelly was bored and had dropped off to sleep. Mom, as usual sensing what I was thinking, turned, saw me and I gestured like I was driving a car. She nodded, yes, and upon finishing their last drinks, they came out of the bar. It was very foggy and damp outside. We walked gingerly but were able to find the car on Palm where we parked.

Basil drove south on Palm to Pacific Coast Highway, turned south to Torrance Boulevard, I think. It was so foggy I was not sure where we were. I heard Basil say, "You have to have cat's eyes to see tonight." From my right,

I saw a huge truck coming at us. I grabbed Kelly who was asleep and fell to my left on the floor...

Hospital, Event 17

The following occurred between the Investigating Officer and the staff at the Torrance Memorial Medical Center Hospital:

"How are they doing, doctor?"

"These two are the only survivors, Officer."

"Has he said anything?"

"Better ask the nurses, they won't leave him."

"Thanks, what does he say, Nurse?"

"He keeps muttering words, and physically doing things. He screams, *Kelly, grabs to his right and tries to fall out of the hospital bed to his left which is why we have him strapped in. Then he says, 'Bartender, two more Bourbons and soda;' then, 'Bartender, two more,' then just, Bartender;' and finally he only raises two fingers.*"

"Pretty graphic; tells us exactly what happened; any alcohol reading in his blood?"

"No. And there was no food in his stomach either which is probably why he's alive."

"How so, Nurse?"

"Because he had severe abdominal injuries, and if he had eaten recently, there would have been blood in his abdomen to begin the digestive process. He could have bled out before the paramedics got to him and brought him here."

"When will he be out of the coma?"

"You will have to ask the doctor about that. He did have head injuries."

"How is Kelly?"

"He obviously saved her life. She was asleep when the accident started. She's able to come in to see him, his name is Cole. Oh yes, and a night Nurse says he spoke directly to her."

"What did he say?"

Never trust London.

Mom's Music, Event 18

In what way do I count
The music I've played?

Is there a master metronome?
A rhythmic clock
That ticks and tocks
A metered display
Of my scoring of each day
Each week, a lifetime
Of striving to strike
That magical sound
That ends
This requiem
Of brittle longing, sameness
And loathing?

Oh, in what way do I count
The failings I made?

P. Kaufman

Fragment: Free to Choose: A Novella

"…Feels like I'm all the way back,
Where I come from…"

Feels Like Home, Randy Newman, 1993

Part III
Chapter I

With the help of a neat gal, Chloe Thompson, who I meet near the Marina in Newport Beach we refurnish my new home slowly, because: by agreement, my former husband is to remove all his furniture as soon as possible…which means, *time*. So, room by room, *slowly*, the house at Pelican Vista Estates takes on my personality. We shop at *Biggars*, *Chandlers*, and *Bullocks* on North Main in Santa Ana and at *Higgins* in Orange for a few items the other stores do not stock.

My dad gets the stuff from storage that is in my apartment before I leave for the Navy and moves it to the smaller of the two guest bedrooms where I am bunking until all the new things can arrive for the master bedroom; all the other bathrooms; the living room; the family/TV room; the breakfast area; the second guest bedroom; appliances for the laundry room, the kitchen and flat wear; the dining room and, of course, every day sheets, towels, etc. I even got an automobile in the divorce. Chloe gives me a bunch of everyday things she no longer needs. I do not want to admit, even to myself, but 508 Via Media, Pelican Vista Estates, California, is beginning to look like I'm recreating the home in Beverly Hills before Mom and Dad split.

I conclude also that all I have in mind for the immediate future is to relax, take it easy until I figure out some kind of a daily life. I have enough money to not go back to the law firm, but I miss it and the challenges in the Navy.

Chloe who is a couple of years older than I am reminds me constantly that part of Pelican Vista monthly dues is for membership and use of the Club which has a dining room, swimming pool, card rooms and social events where I could meet people. I tell her emphatically that my list of activities does not include meeting any men. All Chloe said is, "Well what about sex?" I ignore her question but do agree to go to the Club...but to start out, only on a limited basis.

Chloe insists after weeks of not seeing me when I'm shopping to replace Navy underwear, personal lingerie and other stuff that I could at least accompany her to a great tennis club she belongs to, The Feather Palms. She says, "It has a good massage service called *U-Knead-Me* which includes a special, private program for women. The guy who founds *U-Knead-Me* is Rush Hogarth, he only does massages for men, especially rich executives, but on occasion Rush will do an executive's wife."

Chloe makes The Feather Palms sound great with the kind of privacy that women really need at-a-no-men-allowed spa and tennis lessons for novices; so, I go along to check things out. On my second month of visits including wonderful massages I decide to join. Chloe introduces me to her best friend, Janice Morgan, who is a member; she corners me one day and says, "When the timing is right, Alexis, I'll see if I can get Chloe to tell you a wonderful story about Rush Hogarth." That is all she mentions but it is her tone, knowing smiles and 'if you only know the whole story look,' that tells me that the story must be a gossip's dream or have sexual content better than the time Chloe said, 'What about sex, Alexis?'

Months later, one afternoon, Chloe invites me and Janice to her house for after tennis drinks. I am playing a bit better but never think I'll be in the class of Chloe or Jan. After a couple of rounds of Cosmopolitans everyone is relaxing when the doorbell rings. Chloe answers, comes back and says, "It is just the Vista Estates gardener with a question."

Jan said, "Chloe, remember that day when you and I are here after tennis, the doorbell rings and it's Rush Hogarth who is here to give your husband, Hal, bless his heart, a massage. Hal forgets to tell Rush he will be out of town in New Mexico...about some gas wells. And you ask Rush in for coffee and a croissant?"

"Of course, I do, Jan. What a marvelous memory you have that a doorbell ringing reminds you of an event. I'll mix up another pitcher of drinks, and since we are all good friends here, I'll repeat, to some extent, what happens."

Chloe goes to the bar to mix the cocktails, Jan winks at me, but I guess immediately that the story I am about to hear, or some part of it, is what Jan mentions that she wants me to hear.

Chloe begins, "I fell on Jan's court sitting down hard. The bell rings and its Rush Hogarth coming to the house to give Hal a massage. But Hal is in New Mexico and fails to cancel his reservation. As long as Rush is here with his massage table, oils and massage wraps, I ask him to at least come in and have coffee. Later I suggest, can he give me the massage he plans to give to Hal and work out the sore spot at the end of my spine. He is not too keen on this idea, but with Jan here as a chaperone I persuade him to bring in his equipment. After we talk a bit and Rush looks me over with a critical stare, he agrees to go ahead and give me a massage.

"I'm wearing white: a deep, U-neck tank top with narrow straps one of which keeps sliding off my shoulder and I adjust it; matching material tennis briefs with high cut legs; tennis shoes and one of my expensive dress bras, which obviously Rush sees and knows it is not designed for tennis. No doubt, my stretch material tank top and brief, with the bare midriff between them, contributes to his decision to give me a massage.

"I introduce Jan, my next-door neighbor, to Rush and we have a long talk about his business, *U-Knead-Me*, which he says, 'I'm expanding from men only to accommodate women by adding a salon and spa services, basic massage as well as therapeutic treatment for injuries. I have a state license to perform such a specialty.'

"I show Rush my bedroom where he can set his massage table by the sliding glass door that looks out on the patio and there is plenty of light and privacy. He hands me a body wrap and a special spandex, thong panty. I tell, Rush, 'I'll change in the bathroom and take a shower before my massage.' When I come out all set to go, I remember I said, 'I want a full-body massage because I am pretty stiff from all the tennis…also I ask about unscented oil.' Rush remarks 'that is all I use as no male customer wants a perfume smell when he goes back to work after a massage; I'll wash up in the kitchen.'"

After he leaves, I drop the body wrap, Jan, helps me get up on the massage table. When I roll over on my stomach, she covers me up and sits in a chair right next to the massage table, so she can be a proper chaperone.

Rush returns from washing his hands in the kitchen, folds down the body wrap to expose only my neck, arms and back to the top of my bottom. Rush says, "Sing out, Chloe, if I massage too enthusiastically." I know I reply, "Sure, and also if you're too gentle. "I know he will not find any stiffness or unusual stress because I am in too good shape. But why should I turn down the chance for a massage from a professional. In fifteen minutes, all my arms, hands, fingers and back, from the neck down to the top of my butt are done. Rush says, "I'll finish now doing your lower legs and feet but first let me cover you completely from neck to the top of your bottom."

"That is when, Jan, you say you have to leave and ask if there is anything at Neiman's you need to pick up for me. I recall I lifted up off the table to answer using my arms, which exposes my breasts. My reply takes more than minute; Rush gets a perfect view of my super structure. You say, "Ok, you'll pick up my dress and other stuff; also, I'll feel much better after such a great professional massage."

"Does Alexis want to hear what happens next?"

I shout, "You can't stop now."

"Ok first, I'll get more Cosmopolitans."

Now, I kick off most of the body-wrap until it slides off the table. First, I'm completely naked as I'm not wearing the spandex, thong panty; also, I've decided to go ahead with my plan to seduce Rush in the agenda I've worked out and say to Rush, "Don't forget to massage my back, waist, *all* of my bottom; and the sides of my body above the surface of the massage table"; he just stands there, so I say, "Come on, Rush, you've certainly seen a bare-assed, naked girl before, get started."

"You bet" he says; now the *real* massage begins. He puts oil on my back massaging everywhere until he rubs the area on top of my tailbone; pushing upward toward my waist. With his left hand, he's grasping, pulling on each cheek. I recall I said, "That's it, keep it up." I know that is when I'm flat on my stomach but I'm still able to kick off the rest of the body wraps from the table; nothing is covering me in any way. Rush moves his left hand now, reaching under my legs and begins massaging from the top of my thighs all the way downward to my feet.

Second, I remember groaning and saying, "Roll me slightly toward you, Rush, up on my left hip to give extra attention to all of my *tennis* right hip, and lower abdomen". After the roll, I raise my right leg placing it foot-first on the massage table behind my left knee; this expose all of me, everything: breasts, abdomen and pelvis. I roll again, off my left hip, onto my back and say, "Ok you better massage everything now while I'm on my back, just do my *entire* landscape, including legs."

"Right", Rush says.

I say to Rush, at this key point, "Go back, and stress massaging under, and all sides of my legs again". He agrees and pulls me to the foot of the massage table first; after the move, he tells me, "Lift your legs so I can massage each entire leg, one at a time." After this move, Rush is able to rub every part of me. With each area of massage, I know I gasp, shout some, I'm breathing faster, while using my hands to hold my legs in their elevated positions.

Third, I remember saying, "Rush, I can't believe this position I'm in". Finally, I announce, "Rush, I'm moving and hop off the table. Now it's your turn; at least a dozen, or more, climaxes for me are more than fair…U-Kneed-Me, Rush, right now." I toss the top sheet and blanket on my bed aside, push the firm pillows aside and get ready to lie down on the bed. I recall saying, *this is going to be equally exciting for both of us*…but we must start slowly because massage is great but not the real thing".

"I feel Rush kneel on the bed, move my legs apart a bit more, and start". I know I jerk spontaneously at the touching of sensitive areas. Rush, hands on my hips starts to move me backwards and forwards. Each time I move backward toward him, I open more, and everything becomes easier and more rewarding. I now push back as hard as I can because my legs are now at 90-degree angles from each side of the trunk of my body. I feel orgasms happening and we both reacted the same time and lay motionless on the bed. We hold each other.

Fourth, "You go first, use my shower. I'll be along after I relax, lay flat, stretch out and recover".

I see Rush begin to soap himself and from the bathroom mirrors I can tell he is trying to watch me on the bed. He does not know I am doing what my GYN coached me to do; when he turns his back, I take a special diaphragm from my bedside table, insert it to take full advantage of my orgasm timing and to prevent any "flow back". Rush is out of the shower already dry and through dressing when I emerge completely nude from the bathroom. I get him to finish drying me, put cornstarch powder and my special body lotion on me, "Rush, be a dear, and hook the bra for me, use the last, tightest, openings. I'm wearing a black dress for a late cocktail party this afternoon with plenty of décolleté. After I'm hooked up, I lean forward and adjust my breasts into the correct the bra cups. I sit down, squirm into the sheer to the waist pantyhose and have Rush help me into my dress, do the zipper. I know that after my: cool down, relaxing on the bed, the body drying, cornstarch powder, lotion applications, bra hook up and the bra cup breast adjustments, Rush is ready to go back to bed at any time, now, or in the future."

"So, your whole agenda was a cool strategy to get pregnant; correct, Chloe?"

"Yes, you've got it right, Alexis. My plan was a series of four basic choices; how clever of you to understand what is behind, no pun, everything that happens: First, the Teaser massage to bait the hook; Second, Foreplay…the real massage; Third, Intercourse…the real thing to get pregnant; and Fourth, after-play…setting up a possible future."

"You did get pregnant?"

"You bet! I have twin boys, Russell and Harold."

"How do you explain the pregnancy to your husband?"

"When he comes back from his trip in three weeks, I lure him into one of our infrequent sexual encounters. I know from an examination at my GYN's, after sex with Hal, that he cannot get me pregnant…because of his age and impotent sperm. But I want him to have child for his declining years; Hal admired Rush and said, "He is the kind of man, if I ever had a son, Rush is the ideal model of what I want." I consider artificial insemination but have to choose between an unknown donor vs. Rush and doing the real thing. If I'm guilty of doing anything wrong, it is opting for Rush. I love Hal very much but knew I can't wait about having children and as it turned out, neither could Hal. He only lived to see the boys reach age seven. So now, I'm not just a mother alone with two boys. I have a wonderful friend and lover; who I see discretely, the boys take tennis lessons at The Feather Palms, I play tennis, too. I now have a regular love life, only with, Rush, and the boys think of him as an Uncle. Rush loves them and guides them. Most important they have: a stable home, life, school and friends. I recognize some women would say I'm guilty of electing the wrong choice; but I found a way of keeping what I had and also having a way to get what's necessary without losing my dear husband until he dies. Now, there are three of us who know the truth; Rush, guesses at part of what really happened, and I do pray, Alexis, that you will never divulge or say anything about the *love story* you heard today."

"Of course, Chloe, if there is one thing, I am aware of, being a Naval Officer, is that I might know something but I'm not going to betray it. Your private life is safe with me. Also, all of us have lives that are not always smooth sailing; or as veterans in the Navy say, *Fair Winds and Following Seas*…which do not always happen; the motto, of course, is about wanting things to be that way or hopefully they will soon be that way.

"The diaphragm type and size you used was a GYN prescription to aid conception?"

"Yes, everything was: intercourse, remaining flat in bed after, inserting the diaphragm correctly to prevent any 'flowback' of sperm."

So, your agenda had basically a fifth choice, which worked *twice*: twins and a new full life, congratulations."

"Yes, you're right and clever as *usual*, Alexis.

Fragment: Balancing Fate, Ira and Rachel Go for the Jugular

A man's character is his fate. Heraclitus
Loeb Classical Library, *On the Universe, 121*

Commentary

The problem many of us face is that if we have experienced difficulties in our life, we are treated as if we cannot be of much value in what we impart to others. What happens becomes a variation of an American truism, "If you're so smart, how come you aren't rich?" In essence, most of what we say is tainted because we are not 100% successful in every aspects of life... especially *bargaining*. The sadness about much of this is that so few people recognize that you can only be responsible for yourself as to what you believe, what you stand for, your values, your integrity, your commitments, your loyalties, your caring, sharing, etc.. You cannot be responsible for all these matters in others; only be what you are and learn to handle any temporary events inflicted on you by others before you achieve your goal.

Painful Truth: Round 1

It was the best place for our meeting: on the park side, away from the street where the hotel veranda was quiet, bathed in deep shadows from the trees and cooler than out front where heat radiated from the street and traffic which made it difficult to hear.

Ira, ever watchful, arrived early and ordered two lemonades, without any Vodka. He knew Rachel would prefer hers with Vodka, but today was a *plain* lemonade day. Lunch time was about over so the veranda was virtually empty with only a few left and the afternoon drinkers yet to arrive.

Rachel came along from the street-side, front of the veranda, turned, saw me, waved, walked along the veranda toward me, and sat down right beside me. Both of us were quiet except, for a brief greeting, as if hesitant to speak more before the direction, an understanding of the nature of our conversation was established after the events of the recent weeks.

Rachel's brief greeting, in addition to her serious look, telegraphed that she had come to the meeting with Ira with an agenda in mind, but that she was keeping her thoughts to herself; she sipped her lemonade, frowned at no Vodka, and said nothing. Ira waited, also said nothing and sipped his lemonade, too. He figured Rachel would speak first, but only when she was ready; Ira noted Rachel counting on her fingers...and counted eight times. He guessed when the time was right; Rachel tells me about her eight points...soon the list came out:

1. *I had to get out of Arizona with my son Billy.*
2. *That could not be done while we were solvent...I had to be in debt to go home to get help.*
3. *Ira could not get a divorce in Arizona which would require Lewis' approval to take Billy out of the state to South Carolina;*
4. *Consent unlikely when Ira is not likely to spend money, he did not control, when my family could foot the bill, or his Dad, who Ira believes has plenty of money which he should be able to inherit.*
5. *Leaving would put all the everyday work on me and not prevent Ira from achieving his self-fulfillment...he never realized he was following my plan.*
6. *This shifted financial responsibility to me and took Ira off the hook... the only way he would approve Billy and me leaving...my only possible plan.*
7. *And where is Ira now? Living in another state with a gal who has money and all Lewis' art interests are going first instead of compromising with reality control.*
8. *In other words, this is a different story which is about: who conned whom.*

Round 2

So, I said, "What exactly is making you so Angry, Rachel?"

"What makes you think I'm angry, Ira?"

"Lots of things."

"Tell me."

Ira paused before answering: because he had good reasons to believe that the wrong response now would terminate his already tenuous relationship with Rachel, his former daughter-in-law, because he knew he was the kind of person who said what he felt right off and often that was not the wise way to be. Especially if what he said turned out to be painfully accurate and had merit as was usually true.

"Well, Rachel, I thought you were angry because you felt I blamed you for the divorce. Didn't you?"

"How can you believe I was angry?"

"In the past, did I ever give you any indication of 'blaming you' for anything?"

"No"

"Not only that, if I had blamed you about anything would I have continued to come and see you; remember, every time I came to visit I spent most of my time with you and Billy, taking you to breakfast, to lunch, to the market, or to the beach where all three of us built sand castles together; you name it and we did it. Also, I supported how great you were managing being a single mother and working to get my son, Ira, to stick to his promises to stress the new responsibilities of being a dad with more self-goals than his art and money to support it. Would I have been doing all that if I was angry with you Rachel?"

"I suppose not; maybe I was just frustrated by not achieving as much as I thought I should; and that you never got Ira to have more self-control than only self-achievement in art. You never changed him."

"That's not a thing a person, *especially* not even a parent, can do, Rachel...because the time comes in life when children are no longer capable, or willing, except in very special circumstances, to accept suggestions or advice from anyone. Do you recall that part of a conversation Ira and I had when his good friend talked about moving away where his friend was making very good money and Ira turned it down emphatically?"

"I see what you mean; good point…accents my frustration."

"That is a universal truth, or nearly so, Rachel; I can't influence, let alone run, another person's life or feelings and butting into my son's life is sheer folly and would reinforce his current habit of blaming someone else for every mistake he makes because he never learns from experience. Ira has to make his own decisions, but that does not mean I'm not available when either of you, usually you, Rachel, decides to ask me something, right?"

"Correct, that's true and you would give us your thoughts, ideas, Ira, and often a few of the times when you asked for my experience, Rachel, you or Ira had already made a decision and acted upon it; unfortunately my response to your query was opposite to your prior action."

"That's not fair, Ira, name one instance."

"Ok, how about the supervisor job you wanted, Rachel, and how you handled it?"

"Oh yes, I did blow it and didn't get the job. I should have asked you about your experience first before I acted."

Rachel looked down and despite her usually cheerful and upbeat appearance she looked as if all of the frustrations she had recently spoken of, and now with seven years of marriage to Ira included, everything seemed to be passing before her eyes with the realization you can't marry someone on the basis of changing them. She concluded, "Ira is Ira and always will be and that is no one's fault is it I but Ira's?"

"I'm not sure what you're asking me, Rachel?"

"It's about Ira's personality."

"That's not what we've been talking about; we were talking about your belief of an appearance of Anger with you, on my part and who was responsible for the divorce…and discussing whether a feeling about anger was justified or not, but maybe, we have been really examining Lewis and his battle with an apparent life-long fate of either *Self-Fulfillment* or *Self-Control*. Let me be clear, Rachel, I can't change either you or Ira…each person can only be responsible for their self. And I do not blame you for the plan you had to make and execute to leave Arizona."

"And what does that mean, Ira?"

"It means you chose to leave and it also means that I understand some, but not all, of course, of what happened and what you had to do to get out, Rachel and that also means I don't fault you for what you did."

"What is it you think that I did?"

"Oh, Rachel, you maneuvered to go home to Charleston where you had the support of your family, and finally, some financial security. But it means too, you moved the ball game to your home park where you had a better chance to call the shots; in short, Rachel, you had more control. Most important, by going home you were able to take Billy where he would be sure he could be with you and where you had a job teaching school: you were a divorcee where you used to live and were protected so that you, and especially Billy, could not be taken out-of-state without proper agreements signed by everyone, right?"

"Yes, that's all true."

"Why is it all *true*, Rachel?"

"Because I thought you didn't know, Ira, the extent of the mess Lewis and I were in and, therefore, I feared that you were angry with me and not sympathetic toward me and therefore my actions—you jumped to conclusions."

"Go on, dear."

"I felt I'd lost control of everything that I might have had in the future and you were angry with me because you did not understand all of what had been happening; especially because Lewis and I were in so much financial trouble and sinking so fast it was hopeless."

"Explain that more."

"Well, all our money was gone; we were stone broke, and Lewis was out borrowing, finagling everywhere and figuring his father, you, would be pressured to come to his rescue. We even owed my family, too."

"How could all of your resources have been used up?"

"Because like nearly all young married couples I know, Ira, they have a joint bank account—and one puts money in while the other takes it out?"

"Do you mean all the profit from the sale of the house you bought with your grandfather's wedding gift to you is gone because it went into a joint account?"

"Yes, all of it; where else could it have gone and now it's all been spent and Lewis claims it's because I bought so much stuff for myself and our new baby which is not true—I had one maternity dress for teaching at school and a crib for Billy plus s few baby clothes I did not get as gifts from both sets of grandparents."

"You could have gotten a separate account just for you."

"Oh, Ira, that's something you know about, but I didn't even think of anything like that; I had to believe in Lewis and he could self-manage instead of going on a spending binge: for a new camera and equipment, clothes, tools and even a new pick-up truck. And are you saying, also, that I failed again?"

"Not really, Rachel, but it's a mark of wisdom to recognize that failure to face an issue squarely solves nothing, it only wastes time."

"But, Ira, I'm not that strong—I couldn't go up against Lewis on the question of money and how he spends it with his attitude that whatever I have is his too. Did you?"

"That's a good question, Rachel, and it deserves an honest answer; the truth is that I was in the very same position that you are describing now with you and Lewis—but you are a wife-husband situation and not in a parent-offspring relationship situation. When Lewis grew up and started life on his own, it became obvious that I could just give up, stop trying, and, I guess, I could just step back and walk away from the issue."

"You mean, in a way, just like I did?"

"Yes, that's true. But, be sure to recognize that I was not angry at anyone, especially myself, about the action I took; I told him, 'you're old enough now, you're on your own.'"

"Yes, but isn't a father saying to a son, 'you're old enough now, you're on your own', different than the position a wife is in; she can't say that and become the partnership you talked about a while ago?"

"That's correct, Rachel; and I repeat no one is blaming you. Don't let your fears color your perception: you did what you had to do. And always I felt when I visited everyone in Charleston that you had your feet solidly on the ground."

"Ok, but I felt you were so darn perfect at everything and as a result there was an implied criticism of me."

"Did you feel that way when you asked me to hold Bill when we went to his well-baby checkup and inoculations?"

"No, I loved that you agreed to come with me and made me feel secure; I believed Billy would be safe in your arms and that I could count on you plus I did not want to watch the inoculations—I was chicken to do that."

"That's very honest, kind and loving, Rachel."

"So how can I feel that loving toward you one time, and be angry another?"

"Because we all are human, Rachel, and I think you have seen, understood from all that we are talking about that others can neither establish nor just change your self-esteem; only you can do that. So, what it means is that you are stronger now and understand quite a bit more than when you got married."

"Did you think that I felt otherwise sometime?"

"Yes, but not anymore; we have had a wonderful time together, and you will be a super mother for Billy meeting any challenge that will now seem like nothing more than usual every day events. But another point, you tend to repeat yourself without explaining what you mean—for example, my ability ends up, in your mind, as criticism of you."

"I guess I'm not very good at sorting out what I feel, explaining it without being very sensitive and defensive about it; and at that moment, too, my insecurity took over and that made me think you were upset with me."

"Then, Rachel, I personalized all that was happening and, really, became more upset with myself than angry about anything like what I was saying, thinking or judging."

"What else do you mean, Ira?"

"Some men, Rachel, think that because they earn money it is more important than what the wife does and they down-play the wife's contributions. This is not true and that is what I mean. Women are often more creative than any second level event in the workplace."

"Ok, but how do I get rid of the negative feelings I had about all this, even about you sometimes, Ira?"

Round 3

"That is totally up to you, Rachel, but we are sort of talking in circles and I would like to go back to a comment you made early on: you said Lewis blamed you for spending too much money and therefore are responsible for, to some undefined degree, of both of you being in debt and sinking fast. Lewis has always had a character trait that he needs a constant flow of Newness in his life which is brought on by his aversion to what I call

Sameness. Ira addresses his desire by constant shopping for the "adult toys" common for men to purchase...ones you mentioned were: cameras and all necessary equipment, tools and trucks...you left out everything needed to pursue their favorite hobbies, for Ira, art supplies. Now, how do you get rid of negative feelings? When certain events occur, *like blaming you for the very thing the blamer does himself you have to dismiss it and not let it color your reactions*...I know, easier said than done. After the recent events in your life, Rachel, you are aware of solutions. You are only responsible for you and have to work out responses...you cannot change others."

"Once in a while, all of us to tend to repeat what we talked about, like today, so don't be offended if I say something I have covered already, Ira. One problem, many of us face is that if we experience difficulties in our life, we are treated as if we have little value in what might say to others. It becomes a variation of an American Truism, 'If you're so smart, how come you aren't rich?' In essence, most of what we might say is tainted because we have not been 100% successful...especially if the topic is inter-personal relationships.

"The sadness about much of this is that so few people recognize that you can only be yourself: what you believe, what you stand for, your values, your integrity, your commitments, your loyalties, your caring, sharing and the like. You cannot be a source of similar versions of these characteristics of yours in others."

"That's quite a mouthful, Ira."

"Indeed, it is, Rachel; say more, Ira."

"In a nutshell, 'you are what you are,' and in your words to me, Rachel, you have been hinting about what Love is, so, I will talk about that as reality."

Round 4 - Love, Human Nature

"As you so know, Rachel, mature love is not adapting to, accommodating actions for: compliance with, yielding to every request, passiveness, patronizing or financial dictation. It is rather an understanding of what a person is rather than what we have been told they claim to be; then we find out what they really are." Mature love also understands it goes beyond our needs and concerns. As it has been said: "Love exists when another person's security and satisfaction are as important to you as yours are to you."

"Finally, we must be willing to make the transition from Romantic love with its often essentially selfish wishes and desire such as Lewis has, to proceeding to enduring love and affection that is unconditional and unselfish; renewed constantly through realism and self-control. This transition occurs when caring moves from a love that is purely self-sustaining to commitment; in addition, lovers who are friends have everything after physical love is less urgent; they have mutual openness and acceptance that guides them to a better understanding than only one's physical love... friendship is based on understanding, acceptance, knowledge that money and marriage are desirable but no antidotes for the pain of old wounds or disappointments. You are responsible for healing yourself, but mates always can provide support but without being able to erase past experiences that may have led to feelings of inadequacy. We are cautioned we must first learn to like ourselves or we will never be able to truly able to love another."

Round 5-Control

"Ira, do you know what it is like to be held responsible for all sorts of things over which we have no knowledge let alone control...whatever control means. And to be in that sort of a position for as long as you can remember. Also, to be held to perform at an error free, perfect levels than to be scorned as a perfectionist, or in anther moment to be sought out as the perfect problem solver of other's problems and then, almost concurrently, scorned as a know-it-all who must have any problem solved his way or not at all?"

"When that happens, Rachel, it is time to walk away...absent yourself from the person setting a trap for you...this person who sound like one of those questioners at a political debate does not want the question answered but wants to damage or remove you from the debate at any cost.   •

"Rachel, I can't imagine Lewis ever changing his personality from Self Satisfaction to Self-Control, so you were in the position that you exercised the only possible option available to you when you moved home to South Carolina. You made a sound choice so forget the past."

Fragment: The Interdisciplinary Nature of Marriage

You can watch over people, but you can't make choices for them because Conditions of Psychological Learning and Common Sense are time sensitive are always changing.

The Teeter-Totter

Psyche balanced
Trust and Love
In a union
So tenuous
That a glance
Deed or conjecture
Did injure beyond repair
The bond that had fused
Them together,
So, the first to falter
Was Trust
SoLove
Did then implode
And as their sky
Burst from bright to bleak
It left only
Perpetual disbelieve
In each other.

Peter Kaufman

Fragment: Rules

1. Continuity: Learning is accelerated when a promised reward follows as soon as possible after the pledged reward follows as soon as possible after the pledged reward is made.
2. Effect: Response to a situation which satisfies most individuals equally.
3. Forward association: the sequence in which ideas are naturally linked and easiest to associate and recall later.
4. Exercise: the more a certain response to a situation is repeated, the more likely it will occur again later in an identical situation.
5. Belongingness: ideas, objects naturally related and organized into a meaningful relationship, are more easily remembered than illogical pairings.
6. Therefore: Interference: (negative learning or un-learning) is when one is accustomed to responding in a certain way to a given stimulus and the response to that stimulus is changed; interference occurs…a trading down phenomenon.
7. Intensity: People tend to learn more quickly and better under of conditions of positive emotional arousal.
8. Generalization occurs: when a choice must be made among several responses when alternate responses are available for *the first time*, and the response approximates a satisfactory answer in a parallel language that can be selected (from prior Dating, Pre-marriage when experience,) and generalization is taking place.
9. Repetition: repeating will increase learning and memory of when another, prior similar situation was successfully solved, and success prevailed without acrimony…

10. Distribution of effect principle: a micro builds up, a little each day, is superior for agreement rather than a practice of crash or surprise efforts.

11. Controllable vs. non controllable events; often financial in our Welfare Culture...may become sources of Continuous harm-full Stress.

12. Reread the Essay Introductory Poem concerning *injury* beyond repair.

13. Patience: seldom observed in our explosive, high speed culture.

14. Avoid waste of Time which can be identified as the Deadliest Sin for man because life is finite just as Time is; and procrastination is often felt to be a form of Control.

Fragment: Happy People

Introduction

1. The only happy people I know work at something they consider important.

2. The trouble with most youngsters, they believe a kind of lightening stroke will hit them on the head suddenly without their doing anything. They all seem to wait passively for it to happen without any effort on their part. My impatience has been predominant because they have no stubbornness, no persistence, frustration, tolerance or observation: what do adults expect of youngsters addicted to TV?

3. The only way to be an artist is to work, work and work: the happy people, in item # 1, therefore, are working, hard at whatever he or she enjoys. Success is not a random event that just occurs.

4. Creative people love their tools and materials.

5. An easy fact for self-esteem becomes part of what is important. Observation: this is becoming increasingly hard for average individuals who have seen their livelihoods destroyed by financial manipulators that have invaded and infected our economic reality the past decade. Financial raiders take no responsibility for their actions; only for the fortunes they amass for themselves at the expense of many others. Perhaps some new objective is needed as older concepts of careers with a single organization may return since the forgotten concept of a career with a single organization, over many years, continues to be a thing of the past. Refer to item 6.

6. A prominent management writer's principle will work, but only at the top of the hierarchy of human development which, ideally, the person who was satisfied in basic needs in the past while growing up, and who is now being satisfied in his or her current life situation with safety-needs gratified, not anxious, not fearful, not alienated, not ostracized, will work now if he or she is not orphaned outside the group; but he or she will fit into the group, the team, society. He or she especially have needs when planning a marriage; not a common occurrence in our society as, on the unconscious level, there is not enough feeling of self-love, self-respect, for example, at the, CEO, position where often it's just money and greed that appears to fulfill human needs. In essence, much of the preconditions are just plain baloney. My experience confirms this; I've known two CEOs, who consequently headed two *organizations*, founded by human beings and these two same CEOs destroyed them both while blaming others, the general economy, the new administration but pocketed wealth on the sale of each bankrupt present organization to its new owners.

7. Observation: The point, understand that one must look behind, beneath the surface: do the vetting, an English expression, before buying. He now goes on to list what must be in order. Imagine, if you will, a CEO passing a conference room with a glass outer wall visible partition which one can glance through and see senior officers attending a meeting; now in process, and the CEO turns to you and said, "Watch me interrupt and totally ruin their meeting." He barges into the meeting, interrupts, takes over the meeting and does just what he said he would do. Who is surprised then, some few years later when the company failed?

8. Assumptions underlie Good Management Policy. Look into noted management writings by famous consultants and read their necessary preconditions...which for success include:
A. Everyone is to be trusted: People selected are fairly evaluated to be mature, relatively healthy, descent:
B. Everyone is to be informed as completely as possible of facts and truths as possible, relevant to the situation...knowing is good for people:

C. Your personnel want to achieve and have the impulse to improve; Be sure to select personnel based on these principles, also:

D. There is no dominance, subordination hierarchy in the jungle sense or authoritarian sense: where the jungle view of the world prevails so eupsychian management is practically impossible; it follows, therefore, that this is another principle of selection of personnel: Authoritarians must be excluded, or they must be converted.

E. Everyone will have the same ultimate managerial objectives and will identify with them no matter where they are in the organization or in the hierarchy...this is problem centered rather than ego centered, i.e. "What is best for the solution of the problem or the effectuation of the goal, rather than what is best for an ego or just my own wish." An aside: have rarely, if ever, seen this. As a consequence, most sub organizations within a larger organization are weak. Hence the organization is weak.

F. Eupsychian economics must assume goodwill among all the members of the organization rather than rivalry or jealously

G. Synergy is also assumed. The resolution of the dichotomy between selfishness and altruism is identified: *we normally assume that the more one has the less the other has.* Example, among the Blackfoot Indians, to discover a gold mine, means all prosper from the efforts of the one. In modern society, finding a gold mine is the surest way of alienating many people, even those close to us. If I wish to destroy someone, I can think of no better way...than to give him or her a million dollars. Only a strong and wise person could use this wealth to advantage. Many would undoubtedly lose their friends, family, and everything else in the process of inevitably losing the million dollars, also;

H. Individuals involved are all healthy enough:

I. The organization is healthy enough (Define what that means) and have markets that have reasonable market shares.

9. Believe the "Ability to Admire", to be purely objective not only about other people's capacities and skills, but also about one's own traits.

10. We must assume that the people in the business are not fixated at the safety-need level they must be relatively anxiety-free not fear ridden, have courage to overcome their fear; on the whole, *where*

fears reign, eupsychian management is not possible. In this case, or in many other instances, management experts lack awareness or knowledge of psychopathology of evil, weakness, or bad impulses. Observation: Many have worked for more than one boss whose entire theory of supervisory management was to create an atmosphere of fear.

11. Assume an active trend to self-approve freedom to effectuate one's own ideas, to select one's own friends and kinds of people, to grow, to try things out, to make experiments and mistakes, etc.

12. Assume that everyone can enjoy good teamwork, friendship, good group spirit, good group harmony, good belongingness and group love. Moreover, group love, group identification. Beware of stressing only autonomy...actualization of the individual self.

13. Assume hostility to be primarily reactive rather than character based, like Bubba, being simply honest, let people express irritation, disagreement, etc.

14. Assume that people can take it and can benefit from being stretched and strained and challenged once in a while; that must be only once in a while...not constant.

15. Eupsychian Management assumes that people are improvable. Not perfect but better than they are by a little bit. Observation: a positive orientation based on the pluses these assumptions set forth.

16. Assume that everyone prefers to feel important, needed, useful, successful, proud, respected rather than unimportant, interchangeable, anonymous, wasted, expendable, or disrespected. Assertions that esteem needs, and self-esteem needs are universal, institutionalized. How many have worked for a CEO who expressed the belief that people were just like furniture...if necessary, you simply got rid of them and got new furniture. They were simply interchangeable...sometime later this company went out of business, run by this CEO into the ground.

17. Moreover, everyone prefers, or even needs, to respect, admire... rather than hate the boss; an assumption that certain consultants overlook. Observation: this is a very significant point in regard to the current fuss over harassment; for example, the data about women's sexual responses to men that they regard as strong or weak

are pertinent here: for instance, women may regard, in this context, as having two conflicting impulses toward any male. The first is to see if he can be dominated or used or pushed around. If he can be, then he may be useful but will not be a suitable sexual partner and also, perhaps, never respected as a leader

18. So, assume that everyone dislikes fearing anyone but prefers fearing to hating the boss; the tough and hard but capable leader may be hated, disliked, but is preferred to the soft, weaker leader who may also bring about disaster to continuous employment.

19. Eupsychian Management assumes everyone prefers to be a prime mover rather than a passive helper; the prior condition being a trait, for the more mature, the more healthy; but this is not for all workers throughout the whole organization; that is, not a prerequisite for the entire organization...an assumption for, often, good team work.

20. Assume a tendency to improve things...to clean up any dirty mess, to put things right, to do things better now and to do things better continuously in the future. Good management advice, but it assumes it exists as a prerequisite for success if it exists at all.

21. Assume that growth occurs through delight and through boredom. However, once a delight is experienced long enough it becomes boredom. Then, the individual passes on to a new delight and the cycle repeats so that the search begins anew for additional variety; work at a higher level of skill, and so forth.

22. Assume preference for being a whole person and not a part, not a thing or an implement, or toll, or 'hand:' use all capacities, resistance, as in the highly developed woman, to being *only* a sexual object. (Observation: prearranging of the woman's lib movement, that is.)

23. Assume the preference for working rather than being idle: for the ideal worker, to take away work (life's mission) would be almost equivalent to killing him/her which is contrary to the implied notion in our society that labor is unpleasant, by definition, and enjoying yourself means lying in the sun and doing nothing. Observation: this rule 23 brings home the devastation that has hit so many of our senior level work force which has become unemployed because of mismanagement; tax laws that favor debt while discourage entrepreneurs. We are the only industrial country with a capital

gains tax. We are stifling the creative energy of our most capable people at a frightful cost to all sectors of our society. All in the name of fascism, entitlements and screwball ideas that sap initiative.

24. Most human beings…prefer meaningful work to meaningless work; so, if work becomes meaningless, then life comes close to being without purpose. Observation: Note, people you know who have no real purpose in life, travel on expensive cruise ship, go endlessly to social lunches/dinners, charity events, cocktail parties, etcetera to occupy time with an 'activity.' Therefore, to stop would mean facing a crippling human condition for the affluent: sameness.

25. Assume the preference for individuality, uniqueness, self-identity (in contrast to being anonymous or just an interchangeable entity.)

26. We must make assumptions that people are courageous enough to conquer fear, have stress tolerance (but not to overload status) not psychopathic. And a person must have a conscience, be able to feel shame, embarrassment, sadness, or chagrin, and how people may react to others. Observation be aware of senior officers who have no conscience, no feelings or are even utterly ruthless…would fire someone simply to put another 25 cents more on the profit line… for no purpose other than pure dislike, hate.

27. We must assume the wisdom and efficacy the wisdom of self-choice: this is not true for all levels of workers and must be tempered for those capable of handling it. Nor is it true in all circumstances; people must be selected and screened based on management principles that they can carry out.

28. We must assume that everyone likes to be justly and fairly appreciated, especially in public: praise when due, and don't let false notions of modesty and humility stand in the way of letting a person express accomplishment.

29. We must assume that defense and growth for all these positive trends listed for every good trend in human nature there is also a counter trend;

30. So that everyone, but, in particular, the more developed personalities prefer responsibility to dependency and not passivity most of the time…but not to overload. Too much responsibility can make a person weak; as an example, put on a child's shoulders

too soon in life can cause anxiousness and tenseness forever after. Observation, this is one of the themes as noted by John Bradshaw, the well-known psychologist, who writes on codependency and dysfunctional families.

31. The general assumption is that people get more pleasure out of loving than they will out of hating beware of neurotics and psychotics in whom the pleasure of hatred and destruction are greater than the pleasure of friendship and affection.

32. Assume that well-adjusted people would rather create than destroy.

33. Therefore, well-developed personalities would rather be interested than trapped in Sameness. From this, Maslow, I conclude, talks about many management consultants who, for the most part, talk in far too general, authoritarian type tones, crack the whip where only fascist, fearful, people are successful...critics cite such environments as successful. (Countries such a Columbia, Venezuela, Iran and Syria spring to mind.)

34. Also, observe, that much of the difficulty in the conception of profit, taxes, costs, and ringing the last cent out of an organization which is a target for take-over, is the financially trained executives who are in charge and they are the ones who force upon an entire organization the atmosphere, the aura, of 'Loot and Leave', and that people are nothing more than inter changeable parts and that the real management rationale is all a manager need know is what the top guy wants and just do it...the sooner the better after the top guy sells out his real prize and vanishes.

35. 'Marriage. It unites man with God through the present, just as religious regard for the forefathers unites man with God through the past. Vladimir Solovyov, *The Justification of the Good, An Essay of Moral Philosophy*, English translation, 1918, N.A. Puddington, The Macmillan Company

Yesterday's Wind

'Once upon a time,'
The fable begins
Then weaves, spins
A tale of Princes,
Knights, Squires:
Those who dare
And perform such deeds
As we call, 'Untrue.
Simply impossible to do!

So, cautious, hesitancy bound
We mistrust our opportunity
Our cause our goal,
But then gathering spirit
Reflecting anew,
We posit possibilities pondering
Yet again, again, and again
But a ship doesn't sail
With yesterday's wind.'

A Cancun Theorem

One, add one, lasting
Two, add hype, fleeting
Absent its ethical norm.

Pervasive reality reveals
Persistent correct form,
Adds loyalty, conformity
For mathematical symmetry.

Fragment: Ideas and Images

Prologue

I've been depressed for a period of time since early in June in 1989 so by September I decide to enroll in more classes at the nearby Junior College for a further change of scene. First, I need to examine what is wearing me down and see what, if anything, I can do about it. Since a new CEO took over in January a couple of years ago all the news is bad. Obviously, it appears there is little on the surface that can be fixed, moreover, because some of the best new people have already left which makes things worse and forces middle management to try to support a sinking ship. A careful review of every facet of our operation reveals the new CEO's motive; he micromanages, especially where lower level employees are employed; meanwhile, his micro successes, which collectively amount to macro mistakes, are killing the company. Part of the problem is he believes no one else, but him, is able or competent. Therefore, he always dismisses the experience level of what he considers the lower level, which, by definition, are inferior employees. What I face is his idea that cost reduction by firing lower wage employees is a positive cost reduction that improves profit margins, but he is really increasing production failures with the loss of skilled employees necessary to achieve desired results. Second, another problem for me is the state is taking my backyard for the expansion of a new Freeway. The new right-of-way will be right outside my living room window. Yes, I'm depressed.

So, I chose a new program: continue the Poetry class another semester, add a two-semester class in Short Story structure and writing and plan to take a new program, to begin in the second semester of 1990, a Philosophy class to be called The Theatre of Ideas; everything to be taught by senior level teacher named, Lee Mallory.

Part 1

"Good morning; today we have a surprise guest speaker for our last class before Christmas vacation instead of our regular poetry curriculum. Let me introduce a writer who will impart wisdom, guidance and surprise hints you will not forget as you learn how to improve your poetry and other writing. Since time, our most precious resource is so limited, please no questions. Feel free to take notes, however, and in our classes after Christmas vacation, we will discuss at length today's lecture; your observations, ideas, thoughts, and especially whatever images come to mind, which I look forward to hearing about. Please welcome my longtime friend and famous writer, Ray Bradbury."

"Thanks for the intro, Lee, and it's great to be here again to speak to poets. I can see from the type of students in front of me that you are still attracting mature, motivated people, so, let's get started: first of all, I'm an idea animal not a Science Fiction writer. You are in this class to learn how to make do…accomplish things. And have fun while doing it; positive fun. I hate the doomsters, so I always tell them jokes to loosen them up. Understand, much of what I will say to you is in telegraphic style and it will be up to you to sort it out. Ok, your memories are a resource for you to use; it's how to retrieve them, the memories, are the key. I'll help you do it. One of the answers is friendships, all kinds of them, from relationships to acquaintants: I'm sure each of you has a unique definition of relationship as well as friendship and its friendships which help us sustain our loves not get rid of them; what we want to get rid of are people who doubt us; they are your enemies, not your friends. Don't think of candidates for the honor during our time together, but what I can mention is how to treat negative doubters who want to drag you down.

Next, be aware of what I call cross-pollination; no matter what your field of interest, all your experiences, thoughts, memories and interests transfer into and influence everything about you. For example, I'm reading a poem with Lee that we will give out after class to illustrate my point…I'm not doing it out now because it would interrupt our thoughts as each of you stop to read and analyze it. The poem is by one of Lee's students and may also be included in one of the poems you have discussed so far in this class: the poem is called *Chance and Choice.*

We all need to ask ourselves, 'What roots do we have?' This will help trigger memories, or if you like, another of my terms, 'What will a mid-wife type exposure do for the recall process?' For instance, maybe you recall December 7 1941, (and today is December 7th) and that starts to bring back all sort of memories of what you thought you had forgotten...for me I was doing a play for John Huston called Moby Dick around that time and that brought back all sorts of memories as well as passions of both those moments. However, concentrate on where you are now and take notes for later use.

So, here we are and what sort of mid-wife process can each of you perform to help yourself with memories, passions and the like? This can be done with word association, too, so make list of words then write paragraphs using the words. But remember, this must be a work of fun...and you can also use colors, music and/or the lyrics that go with the music. All of this helps make you a keen observer as well; be aware, too, that often as one writes things come out which are a complete surprise. It happens to me. Now a word of caution, don't push the memory thing, let it occur quietly as you are mining years of the subconscious-well that is inside you. This dredging is almost like meeting yourself.

My scope of interest is vast; I write every day and have for 65 years and have watched the ideas my head links together as I play with them; and to repeat, it's like meeting yourself. When you do this, be alert to happenstance...which means, especially what is happening by chance, and you just let it transpire. More examples: I read a poem, an essay or a short story every night which builds my bank of ideas. I just let it percolate in my brain and when I write, it bursts out...actually, I'm simply teaching myself. I will move on, time is limited; your emotions make you survive, then your intellect takes over. I learn from all media: go to art galleries, plays, read everything...even the comics which I've cut out and have saved for years. Just be alert to any place ideas can come from and do it with joy and fun; I never miss any movies and I love Garry Larsen.

Find someone who *loves* you for what you *are* and what you *do*, has intuition; it's done much for me and my creativity...just plunge ahead, do not worry about what you are doing or where you are going, trust your intuition. A word of caution: part of you is private, so do not talk about it. Remember as well: every love affair is a journey, a mystery, an enchantment; and that human work sustains, not political, not religious.

Some final thoughts: things must be fast, if you slow down, you can ruin things; dry spells come from doing what you should not be doing; your body is telling you to do something else which might be to stuff yourself with data/background to do what you are now attempting. So, be extra alert to any place ideas can come from, also understand you must make a profit (perform) or go out of business.

It's been wonderful talking to you, thanks, Lee, and good luck poets and success in your writing; you have been a great audience."

We all expressed our appreciation to Mr. Bradbury for his time and the lecture by standing and applauding. Lee said, "Ray and I are on our way to lunch in the faculty dining-room; he has to leave very quickly and will not have, as I pointed out, any time to answer questions. However, in our next classes we will discuss Ray's presentation and I expect complete cooperation from everyone in the discussion. Be sure to pick up your copy of the poem, *Chance and Choice*. See you all after Christmas vacation on Thursday January 4th, 1990."

The surprise lecture was my last class for the day except for low impact aerobics in the swimming pool. Since I was the student who wrote, *Chance and Choice*, I did not need a copy but collected a copy anyway; however, I found that Lee and Bradbury were looking at another of my poems, too, *The Song;* so, after aerobics, I just went home with copies of both poems.

Chance and Choice

Chance and Choice skipping along
Detoured, sat either side of me.
Chance's entreaties spoke to my soul
Of uncertainties, hopes, goals,
That friends, tell friends.
"Choice," I said,
"Can you assure my
Wishes come to pass?"
"Alas," she warned,
"Each his fate must cast
In hand to touch, lips to kiss
Body to caress, be caressed,
But pray, pray,
From the lovers Chance sends,
You chose the friend."

The Song

What is your apprehension?
Why not sing to her desires
Knowing that
Whatever the dimension
Of those fires,
To deter
May only lessen her desire?

But I did commit, just so,
And now, how can you know
The angst I feel
Having sung
Her song,
Only to find
Her gone?

Part 2

I gave my attention to the lecture and Ray's statement that he's an idea person not a Science Fiction writer. I think I understood that the ideas he collects he then uses and makes them into important elements of his stories. Maybe some of the ideas, often, form the background, for part of the plot; the location or the time period of a story. In other words, it's ideas which stimulate him, and his imagination takes over from there. It's really that he hasn't experienced everything that is in a story but it's this collection of ideas which his imagination and talent use to create and turn it into the final product.

So, I got out one of my loose-leaf, three-hole binder notebooks and began to analyze my notes, tie them together and see how my efforts might be reflected in images in any poems I'd already written or any future writing I might do. I detected how being organized about writing 'ideas and images' could lead to, maybe, a single story or even two; and I did need help because I'd just accepted an assignment to be the Class Agent responsible for a yearly letter devoted to fund raising. Moreover, even early in my thinking about the job I'd taken, I decided I would not write anything usual but would try-out current topics and make them apply to the importance of fund raising to achieve objectives for the accomplishment of goals not just the grandeur of who raises the most money. (How true my thoughts turned out to be: after 25 years of off-beat letters for the Annual Fund, I turned many of my ideas into short stories. I called them: *Road Coffee, Fragile* and *The Bank of Dad*... just three of the 45 stories in my five published books.) But that's another 'story;' it's back to Ray Bradbury's lecture, the notes I took at the lecture and the entries I made in the loose leaf binder books that I filled with the analysis and what I put together from what I believe Ray Bradbury meant in his telegraphic style lecture to all of us.

I put together three of his thoughts: there is cross pollination no matter what your areas of interest or field are; you are here to make things work out, find solutions and how to make do; memories are a resource for you to use, and what I tell you will help you to access and retrieve things; friendships help us sustain our loves, not to get rid of them—however, get rid of people who doubt you: they are not your friends, they are your enemies. This last point made me think *it wasn't some eccentric CEO who made me feel depressed, isolated, it was the people in my private life. They ran down my batteries because they were weak and selfish. They wore away my armor and left me vulnerable and made it seem I was inadequate, not them.So, I asked, why do people pick certain types to be friends with? It was really a question for an experienced psychologist, but indirectly Bradbury triggered it and gave one answer: get rid of people who doubt you.*

The Suitor

That devil Time winked at me
His clock it is that meters the sea.
He bid me, "Wait, be cautious, slow;
Do not the waves in row on row
Always kiss a distant beach?"
So I paused, reflected, did not reach
To touch her lips, her breast, her hand
Nor did I notice on the sand
That Time sat and decoyed the sun
Its downward progress now begun
And before I guessed Time's subtle game,
The watch ran down that held my name.

Verities I

Winds
Of perpetual favor
Fill childish daydreams
Till Harmonia wraps us
In pragmatic arms
To tutor the genuine
Reality of life's game:
The price of pleasure
Always includes
Pain.

Part 3

I noticed how the next Poetry class ended with only a brief discussion of Bradbury's lecture. In fact, I was the only student who gave the lecture any attention; so, I soon decided to stop making any comments. Many poetry students had elected to take the Short Story course and our emphasis, therefore, turned this new class into a discussion of how the writers of the 30s and 40s, as well as some writers of today, all start with short stories before they write novels.

I did notice how Ray Bradbury's lecture uses elements writers should employ which contrast poems with the plots/dialogues of Short Stories. I noted, as well, Bradbury talks to poets where he "appears to be 'farming for fodder' for his stories which while they are, in his words, not *Science Fiction*, they are truly a form of myth/fantasy." Regard, as well, Bradbury ties together rules for writing to illustrate how an author reflects/feels about the *impact* of what Bradbury is saying and how an author chooses poems he has written to illustrate Bradbury's 'hidden meaning—true impact' of his content in the lecture. Some examples:

Be a keen observer

Rid yourself of people who tear-you down, they are enemies

The meaning of cross pollination

Value of money

Value of searching memory for hidden gems in poems

Color/word lists which trigger memory

Music which also triggers memory

Value positive relationships which sustain both

loves, us, and do not destroy; see below.

Value of acting fast before idea/image is lost

What you write and how you play with ideas must be fun.

Also, it may be a surprise for you as my writing and idea-play is for me.

Have a wide array of interests, write every day.

This is only a partial list from his lecture and other matters will be covered as appropriate.

From the above: why do you hang onto friendships that are negative for you? As a possible clue, recall the number of women (not to pick on woman—this example just came to mind) who form Coffee Klatches. What are some of the common character elements among the members of that group? All are angry, all are divorced, all are shoppers, all are gossips, all want their friends who are unhappy with husband, job, home, level of income, marriage, etc. to join the Klatch and to participate in the bitching, etc.

Find someone who loves just you for what you are and what you do. This is easier said than done for the average individual in our culture. Access to the market place of opportunity, things, people, and so forth is not the same for everyone or the *tempted*; some relationships are like TVs, cell phones, VCRs, sexual partners, clothing, and the like; one does not practice loyalty, commitment, maintenance, with those relationships, one throws them out for a new model.

"Oh, what a tangled web we weave
When first we practice to deceive!"
Marmion, Sir Walter Scott, (1808)

The Flirt

Love is the clever one
As she slides easily
Off the tongue
In the moment of passion's
Parting and entrance
Into her dictionary
Of sensual meanings
And sounds,
But it's after the banquet
Of kef exercise and fun,
Where whispered
Alcoholic chatter
Washes the palate
Of your professed,
Joined hip-to-hip,
And tete-a-tete,
That says more.

The Teeter-totter

Psyche balanced
Trust and Love
In a union
So tenuous
That a glance,
Deed or conjecture
Did injure beyond repair
The bond that had fused

Them together,
And so the first to falter
Was Trust
So that Love
Did then implode
And as their sky
Burst from bright to bleak
It left only
Perpetual disbelief
In each other.

Part 4

From my lecture notes, I began to paraphrase and expand some of Ray Bradbury's rapid paced lecture material. At this point, however, he said to us, if I remember it and my notes are correct, 'for your creativity, plunge ahead, do not worry about what you are doing or where you are going with it, trust your intuition'.

I also know he did say, "I am blessed with imagination and intuition and both have done much for me." This made it so clear I thought *a spark of creativity is greater in some than in so many others of us; just like talent… and that while hard work does help, you can't always count on talent which you may not have.* "Sometimes," Bradbury continued, "using one of my memory stimulators will work; for example, *color*, may generate ideas and images especially when I'm writing poetry." "However," as he said in sort of an aside and a cautionary sort of voice, "part of you is private so don't talk about something you do not want to really say and then wish you had been more careful." He did not talk or elaborate on this statement again as if to imply it is up to each of us to decide what is private and confidential and maybe painful experiences will guide us. This is an enigma, too, for me, as writers generally base their output on their life and what they have encountered; how painful some events are that they become too familiar, that perhaps, they should not be mentioned or relived. I know certain family experiences I've been asked to learn and write about which fall into this category. So, should a writer stay away from too sensitive situations that a reader may think reveal more about the author then about a character in the story?

This very enigma came up again when Bradbury said, "Human works, (writings) sustain, not Political, Religious ones." I felt this remark could generate long and heated debate but as a generality, though, I could understand he would seem to be on target to some extent. My notes also include Ray making the point, "things have to be fast to be good; if you slow down, you can ruin things." I thought right away *maybe that could be when you spoke too quickly and wished later you had thought before speaking!*

I understood his comment about speed to apply to a person's writings, not to the *pace* of an author's personal life, but completely to the *specifics* of a writer's day to day written output. I was partly not wrong, as Bradbury continued, "the pace of a story has to build," but for example, he also added, "every love-affair is a journey, a mystery an enchantment." I thought *this was finally one answer of what to keep private.*

I took this part of his comment to describe someone like Bradbury who must have lived on the edge; who had the money to be in the fast lane and never slow down. Also, it would include a Hemmingway typewriter, who has the same type: fast, never slow down, personality.

Harmonia

Myths:

The oblong leaves,
Ripened orange hued fruit
Of the Persimmon
Rustle, sway to the winds
Of perpetual, positive favor
As day paints into night.

Shimmering, dancing
Mirages foretell
Sunsets of mutable
Mandarin, the seafarer
Sights as delightful
Devoid of any affrights.

Verities II

A possum stirs at nightfall
Pulpy, vermillion fruit to eat
As a wondrous necklace
Wind fallen is
Created at its feet.

Harmonia importunes
A red warning:
'Pleasure is never absent pain,
It's the price that euphoria
Keeps hidden
But eventually, everyone pays.'

Part 5

The current last class of Lee's poetry class and Christmas Vacation are next; both items remind me of last year and the surprise lecture by Ray Bradbury. Also, it's the end of the first semester in Short Story structure and writing, and to keeping a diary for the second semester to create a short story for class review and comment. So, I check where I am in my notebook of lecture notes and comments. I'm at the Bradbury topic which is Dry Spells in Creativity which my notes begin with his comment, "Dry Spells come from the writer doing what he shouldn't be doing." I thought *this sounds like it is a two-phase problem; one is creativity and the other is related, in some manner, to the passage of Time, with a capital T. I relate my thought to a story I was working on about a drinking club founded by some infantry veterans who are unwinding, celebrating their survival in another war and now, which seems common, have become oblivious to Time, by all-out drinking designed to blot-out memories. Their program continues until the club's 'top drinker, Ivor Wallace Harker' gets fed up, takes all his clocks into the backyard and begins to shoot, destroy, all of them, with his M11, especially his battery operated one that displays Time's passage in seconds.*

But back to Bradbury who continues his comment by saying, "the writer is in a rut, not moving fast enough, blocked by surroundings in the wrong Time warp, colors, or sounds, like music; but the biggest cause is not moving fast enough and not stuffing yourself with data, or the background, of what the writer must have, to construct what he needs for his story. Also, the writer may lack money because of failure to make profits or just go out of business." Bradbury continues, "You must become passionate for an idea about which you then write," you ask yourself, 'what are your experiences, what event will act like a mid-wife to help give birth to your goal, get in touch with fun in creating'? Have I lost touch with 'writing must be fun,' being a keen observer, believing, truly believing, really seeing and dredging from the subconscious-well inside me, let a biased way of observing filter out what has never occurred to me before; let memory happen to me, but don't force things. Moreover, cultivate the widest possible interests, write every day, the ideas in your head will link together and then you can play with ideas, but it must be fun', to repeat, "what I have been urging you to do." *It is painful, but Bradbury is also saying, Americans: often spend their entire working lives doing something they dislike and, therefore, lack creative juices. Bradbury is repeating himself but is stressing you have to tell your audience three times, or they won't get it.*

I went back to my notes about Time in the story, *Ivor Wallace Harker*, and note Sergeant Harker is telling his buddies, *once Time is burned, it's gone, usually lost forever in memory, especially when Time is not used positively, which is what we are all creating by being drunk every moment of every day and using the lyrics and the music we listen to as augmentation to increase our drinking; our lives, he says, are becoming unreal, illusions.*

Halloween

The simple frights:
Ghouls, goblins, sprites
Must be conquered by maturity
But alas with age
Some still trade the simplicity
Of Halloween's ghosts
For a host of mindless fears
That wisdoms years
Should dissipate.
But we do bargain bogus
Treats and hollow tricks
To contrive a life of delusions,
And when the price is paid,
We ponder our predicament.
And as reality pales, eludes us,
We long for those simpler days
Of jack-o'-lantern illusions.

Tango

Charm did Tango, 'round us
Eluding, tricking with its merry,
Capricious smile, while tempting,
Inviting remembrances of
Lighthearted days, where
Wrapped in each moment, were
Rituals: fun, parties, glorious
Intimate nights of dancing
Grasping,
Hugging, loving and
Time.
Oh yes, wondrous Time
We thought would never end!

Part 6

From rereading my lecture notes, I notice a strong connection between Dry Spells and cramming yourself with data, playing with ideas which can link in your head and first, being alert to Happenstance, discovering the unexpected. Early in his lecture Bradbury even gives us a definition: "what happens, by chance, where you let things happen which gives trust and you can even meet yourself."

I thought of a story I wrote for one of my books some time ago about an English MI5 Agent who solves a puzzle everyone has worked on unsuccessfully. The Agent became lost in the maze of one-way-streets in a small city in western Pennsylvania and stops to have lunch in a restaurant called The Tea Room. A group of similarly dressed people are just leaving but the Agent is in time to observe them. He asks the waitress what the letters WCH he sees on their green medical smocks means. She says, 'Westmoreland County Hospital.' In an instant the Agent knows he has the answer to where the twins he is Vetting were born who were found wrapped, abandoned in West Virginia with blankets with WCH on them. His visit to the local County Hospital confirms everything and leads to solving a complex matter.

This exercise in demonstrating, in pinpointing, an important Happenstance I wrote long before hearing Bradbury's lecture, caused me to note *again* a few more of his advices to every writer: "emotion makes you survive and then your intellect takes over; be alert to any place ideas can come from...media, movies, art galleries, museums, chance meetings, a play, new surroundings, and the like; memory joggers especially words, colors, music, even odors from plants, and so forth". I recall Bradbury speaking about what he reads every night and he mentioned essays. I realize that in my new class, The Theatre of Ideas, we have, so far, written essays on Life, Love, Death, Bliss, and another subject, 'follow your heart's path,' where we reviewed a Frost poem, *The Road Not Taken*, as a starting point.

The Apples of Hesperides

Certainly, they are free!
Look how scattered among
Eden's trees
Unguarded, unattended
They hang
Uneaten save by crows
Which peck at their deep,
Golden glow,
Spoiling at random
Row upon row.
So sprint, Atalanta,
Pursue as your
Desire demands,
Tempts you to gather
A fallen few,
Then fly, fly, fly
Seeing, believing
They are free, free, free,
Except for the slavery
Of Golden Apples.

Seascape

Recall,
When wave spray
Scatters off the rocks
The fragments portray
A prism of colors
In the Autumn sun
And you hurry to capture
A picture's worth
On our picnic basket?

Damn,
You'll never render
The reality you strive for each day
As you repaint, repaint, repaint
Fool,
Spray colors dry
While you chafe, chafe, chafe,
Just like our wetness
Evaporated, too, when your
Control, control, control,
Harried us into arid oblivion.

Part 7

There are two admonitions that Bradbury gives us that quietly depend on key words: he tells us what we want to do is to get rid of all people who *doubt* us: *Doubt* is the key word in this piece of direction; however, it was stressed as he spoke, so I have highlighted it, as I believe he would have were his lecture printed for us. The second instruction contains a pair of key words to find someone who loves you for what you *are* and what you *do*. Both these words are operational and, once again, they were stressed as he spoke, and I believe would have been highlighted in a printed version of his lecture. These instructions impressed me as *imperatives* and are not simple to accomplish, in fact, both tasks will be difficult to achieve.

It was also of interest to me that Bradbury did not speak in his lecture to us about Death or how thoughts of Death can impact, effect writing, mental health and a writer's enthusiasm. As a consequence, I added more of my poems, following, concerning Death; the last one contains four stanzas.

Peter Kaufman

Hourglass

I cannot love you
As a young man
For it is today, and sand
Through my glass
Has flowed
So now I go
At another ardent pace
That only youth can give
Its time to glean.
Nor green, dear, you be
Poised in sexuality
At that edge of genesis
Where all newness grows,
And grows, and grows
Until you know
Our sifted sands
Make still more levels
On which we stand
To love
And see the stars.

Daylight Again

It's tidy up time:
Like dead weeds
That grew abundantly
In the seams
Of sidewalks
During the seed Time of life,
And those horns-of-plenty:
Attics, basements, closets,
Garages, with garment bags,
Boxes, barrels, desks,
Dressers stuffed
With memories, stored strife;
All in categories
From a hair lock
To final supplies:
A cup, water pitcher, bedpan
For that day whose shade,
Some say,
Is but the real
Step to light.

The Skiers' Club

Membership bought in grief
Knits tight, tight sphincters
And concentric wreaths
With printed ribbons that speak
The real rules of our way:
'No Trespass',
'No Entrance',
'No Friction'.
And fear, as in a contagion,
Rears its iron walls, its faction
Around us

Fragile elements
Of Time and Health
Grind quietly in the dark
To dust
And still we trust
Do not see: ski dust,
Makes no shared coffee
On the plaza in the sun
With its bright sky and breezes,
Do look up and heed
That still empty seat

Ski, ski, ski
(Don't catch an edge)
As gusts on slopes
Of Buttermilk
Spray powder
More sour than our
Many skis can churn
And there amid the sunlight's
Split, prismatic colors

Kindred, costumed phantoms
Chase, and chase, and chase the day

But night climbs closer
Curtails the play
Of rainbow festooned ladies
Who race, and race, and race away
As if their new sterile motion
Can stop that avalanche of seconds
And those cucumber sandwiches,
And tea
Eaten
After others
Never after me

Part 8

Addendum

With thoughts of the curriculum in my new class, *The Théâtre of Ideas*, I recalled it included an emphasis on what the teacher, Dr. Eileen Bennet, called a Paradigm Shift or Change; when she spoke about it, she read us a definition: *a philosophical and theoretical framework of a scientific school or discipline within which theories, laws and generalizations and experiments performed in support of them are formulated.*

This she followed with some examples that, to me said, 'cultural change;' which I immediately related to parts of Ray Bradbury's Lecture and his use of ideas and images, or events and results, that he percolates in his mind until he gets a direction and starts to write quickly, as usual, about, say, an *entire New world* like in his novel, *The Martian Chronicles*, which according to the definition we had heard, is a Paradigm Change.

Later, I looked again at the essay hand out Dr. Bennet gave us, I reread it; the title is *Thinking About Women, Men and Social Change, in the 1980s*, and found that Dr. Bennet was definitely writing, and included interviews with both women and men, about changes in our society's set of current images of the roles of women and men in our culture; she believes the images are in the process of undergoing modification: a revolution, or a Paradigm Shift, is taking place. I reviewed my class notes and also reread them: Paradigm flexibility is not always available or accessible in our culture because of failure of individual views of reality and often the proposed new Paradigm strikes at the vested interest of either a large or minor group of people who have, in their vision, a great deal to *lose* by the adoption of a changed culture; unfortunately, it's often only a minor group which has a lot to *gain* by the change, but with proper backing, can exert extreme pressure while being fully unaware of the scope of all side effects of what they want. For example, in social services for the less fortunate we can see political interest in the perpetuation of the process of helping but not in attainment of the goal.

I'm amazed by the similarities between Bradbury's and Bennet's Paradigm Change efforts, however, each is coming with a different direction and focus while their sense of *urgency*, as expressed in their ideas and images of necessary events and results, is uniform. So, I'm including two additional poems that appear after Part 8 which are pertinent.

Yesterday's Wind

'Once upon a time,'
The fable begins
Then weaves, spins
A tale of Princes,
Knights, Squires:
Those who dare
And perform such deeds
As we call, 'Untrue.
Simply impossible to do!

So, cautious, hesitancy bound
We mistrust our opportunity
Our cause our goal,
But then gathering spirit
Reflecting anew,
We posit possibilities pondering
Yet again, again, and again
But a ship doesn't sail
With yesterday's wind.'

Time Starts Now II

Imprisoned
In that umbra
Of prior pain
And its darkness,
Its numbness
That piles
Shadow upon shadow,
Layer by layer,
To blot out

Your evenness
Your energy?
Evolve Hell,
Erupt!
Time Starts Now.

Printed in the United States
By Bookmasters

Printed in the United States
By Bookmasters